1295

D1053130

9f

the attack

Also by Yasmina Khadra
PUBLISHED IN ENGLISH

In the Name of God

Wolf Dreams

The Swallows of Kabul

NAN A. TALESE

Doubleday

NEW YORK

LONDON

TORONTO

SYDNEY

AUCKLAND

the

attack

YASMINA KHADRA

Translated from the French by
JOHN CULLEN

PUBLISHED BY NAN A. TALESE
AN IMPRINT OF DOUBLEDAY
a division of Random House, Inc.
1745 Broadway, New York, New York 10019

DOUBLEDAY is a registered trademark of Random House, Inc.

This book is a work of fiction. Names, characters, businesses,
organizations, places, events, and incidents either are the product of the
author's imagination or are used fictitiously. Any resemblance to actual
persons, living or dead, events, or locales is entirely coincidental.

The Attack was first published in 2005 under the title L'attentat in
France by Julliard, Paris.

Library of Congress Cataloging-in-Publication Data
Khadra, Yasmina.
[Attentat. English]
The attack / Yasmina Khadra ; translated from the French by
John Cullen.—1st ed. in the United States.
p. cm.
I. Cullen, John. II. Title.

PQ3989.2.K386A8813 2005
843'.914—dc22
2005052944

ISBN 0-385-51748-3

Copyright © 2005 by Yasmina Khadra
English language translation copyright © 2006 by John Cullen
All Rights Reserved

PRINTED IN THE UNITED STATES OF AMERICA

2   4   6   8   10   9   7   5   3   1

First Edition in the United States of America

the a t t a c k

I don't remember hearing an explosion. A hissing sound, maybe, like tearing fabric, but I'm not certain. My attention was distracted by that quasi-divinity and the host of devoted followers surrounding him as his bodyguards tried to clear a passage to his waiting automobile. "Let us pass, please. Please move out of the way." The faithful elbowed one another, hoping to get a better look at the sheikh or touch a part of his *kamis*. From time to time, the revered old man turned to greet an acquaintance or thank a disciple. The eyes in his ascetic's face glinted like the blade of a scimitar. I was being crushed by the enraptured throng and tried in vain to break free. The sheikh plunged into his vehicle, waving with one hand from behind the bulletproof glass while his two bodyguards took their places on either side of him. And then . . . but there's nothing more. Something resembling a lightning bolt streaks across the sky and bursts like a giant flare in the middle of the roadway; the shock wave strikes me full force; the crowd whose frenzy held me captive disintegrates. In a fraction of a second, the sky collapses, and the street, fraught with the fervor of the multitude a moment ago, turns upside down. The body of a man, or perhaps a boy, hurtles across my vertiginous sight like a dark flash. What's going on? A surge of dust and fire envelops me, flinging me into the air with a thousand other projectiles. I have a vague sensation of being reduced to shreds, of dissolving in the blast's hot breath. . . . A few yards—or light-years—away, the sheikh's automobile is ablaze. Hungry tentacles enclose it, spreading abroad a dreadful odor of cremation. The roar of the flames must be terrifying; I can't hear it. I've been struck deaf, ravished away from the noises of the town. I hear nothing, I feel nothing; I hover, I only hover. I hover for an eternity before plunging back to earth, stunned, undone, but curiously lucid, my eyes wide open on the horror that has just descended on the town from out of the sky. In the instant when I touch the ground, everything freezes: the flames rising above the destroyed vehicle, the flying projectiles, the smoke, the chaos, the smells, time. . . . Only a heavenly voice, floating over the fathomless silence of death, is singing *One of these days, we'll go back home*. It's not exactly a voice; it's more like a rustling, a filigree of sound. . . . My head bounces off something. . . . A child cries: *Mama!* The call is weak, but distinct and pure. It comes from far away, from some calm elsewhere. . . . The flames devouring the sheikh's car refuse to budge; the projectiles won't fall. . . . My hand gropes among the gravel. I believe I've been hurt. I try to move my legs, to lift my head; not one of my muscles obeys me. . . . *Mama*, the child cries. . . . *I'm over here, Amin.* . . . And there she is, Mama, emerging from behind a curtain of smoke. She advances through the suspended debris, amid petrified gestures, past mouths opened upon the abyss. For a moment, because of her milk white veil and her tormented look, I take her for the Virgin. My mother was always like this, radiant and sad at the same time, like a candle. When she placed her hand on my burning forehead, she took away all my fever and all my cares. . . . And now *she's here*; her magic powers are still intact. A shudder runs through me from my feet to my head, setting everything free and unleashing delirium. The flames start their macabre movement again, the exploded fragments resume their trajectories, and panic comes flooding back in. . . . A man in rags, with blackened face and arms, tries to approach the blazing automobile. Although he's gravely wounded, some reserve of stubbornness moves him to try to help the sheikh, no matter what the cost. Every time he puts his hand on the door of the car, a jet of flames drives him back. Inside the blasted vehicle, the trapped bodies are burning. Two blood-covered specters approach from the other side and try to force open the rear door. I see them screaming orders or crying out in pain, but I don't hear them. Not far from where I'm lying, an old man stares at me stupidly; he doesn't seem to realize his guts are exposed to the air and his blood is streaming toward the crater in the street. A wounded man with an enormous smoking stain on his back is crawling across the rubble. He passes quite close to me, groaning and panic-stricken, and gives up the ghost a little farther on, his eyes wide open, as if he's still denying that such a thing could happen to him, to *him*. The two specters finally break the windshield and dive into the automobile. Other survivors come to their aid. With their bare hands, they pull apart the flaming vehicle, break the windows, tear off the doors, and succeed in extracting the sheikh's body. A dozen arms lift him up, carry him away from the inferno, and lay him down on the sidewalk, while a flurry of other hands strives to beat the fire out of his clothes. A deep, intense tingling makes its presence felt in my hip. My trousers have almost disappeared; only a few strips of scorched cloth cover me here and there. Against my side, grotesque and horrible, my leg is lying, still connected to my thigh by a thin ribbon of flesh. Suddenly, all my strength deserts me. I have the sensation that my fibers are separating from one another, already decomposing. . . . At last, I hear something, the wailing of an ambulance, and little by little, the noises of the street return, break over me like waves, stun me. Someone bends over my body, gives it a summary examination with his stethoscope, and goes away. I see him stoop before a heap of charred flesh, take its pulse, and then make a sign to some stretcher-bearers. A man comes to me, picks up my wrist, and lets it fall again. . . . "This one's a goner. We can't do anything for him." I'd like to hold him back and force him to reconsider his assessment, but my arm mutinies, refusing to obey me. The child starts crying out again: *Mama*. . . . I look for my mother amid the chaos . . . and discover only orchards, stretching as far as I can see . . . Grandfather's orchards . . . the orchards of the patriarch . . . a land of orange trees, where

every day was summer . . . and a dreaming boy on the crest
of a hill. The sky is a limpid blue. Everywhere, the orange
trees are holding out their arms to one another. The child is
twelve years old, with a porcelain heart. At his age, there's
so much to love at first sight, and simply because his trust
runs as deep as his joy, he thinks of devouring the moon like
a fruit, convinced that he need only reach out his hand to
gather up the happiness of all the world. . . . And there, before my eyes, despite the tragedy that has just ruined forever
my memory of that distant day, despite the bodies of the
dying scattered in the street and the flames that have now
completely overwhelmed the sheikh's automobile, the boy
bounds to his feet, his arms spread like a kestrel's wings,
and goes running across the fields, where every tree is
enchanted. . . . Tears furrow my cheeks. . . . "Whoever told
you a man mustn't cry doesn't know what it means to be a
man," my father declared when he came upon me, weeping
and distraught, in the patriarch's funeral chamber. "There's
no shame in crying, my boy. Tears are the noblest things we
have." Since I refused to release Grandfather's hand, my father knelt before me and took me in his arms. "There's no
use staying here," he said. "The dead are dead, they're over,
they've served their time. As for the living, they're ghosts,
too; they're just early for their appointment. . . ." Two bear-
ers pick me up and put me on a stretcher. An ambulance
backs up to us, its rear doors wide open. Arms pull me inside and practically throw me among some other corpses. In
my final throes, I hear myself sob. . . . "God, if this is some
horrible nightmare, let me wake up, and soon. . . ."

I.

_____

After the operation, Ezra Benhaim, our hospital director, comes to see me in my office. He's an alert, lively gentleman, despite his sixty-odd years and his increasing corpulence. Around the hospital, he's known as "the Sergeant," because he's an outrageous despot with a sense of humor that always seems to show up a little late. But when the going gets tough, he's the first to roll up his sleeves and the last to leave the shop.

Before I became a naturalized Israeli citizen, back when I was a young surgeon moving heaven and earth to get licensed, he was there. Even though he was still just a modest chief of service at the time, he used the little influence his position afforded him to keep my detractors at bay. In those days, it was hard for a son of Bedouins to join the brotherhood of the highly educated elite without provoking a sort of reflexive disgust. The other medical school graduates in my class were wealthy young Jews who wore gold chain bracelets and parked their convertibles in the hospital lot. They looked down their noses at me and perceived each of my successes as a threat to their social standing. And so, whenever one of them pushed me too far, Ezra wouldn't even want to know who started first; he took my side as a matter of course.

He pushes the door open without knocking, comes in, and looks at me with his head tilted to one side and the hint of a smile on his lips. This is his way of communicating his satisfaction. Then, after I pivot my armchair to face him, he takes off his glasses, wipes them on the front of his lab coat, and says, "It looks like you had to go all the way to the next world to bring your patient back."

"Let's not exaggerate."

He puts his glasses back on his nose, flares his unattractive nostrils, nods his head; then, after a brief meditation, his face regains its austerity. "Are you coming to the club this evening?"

"Not possible. My wife's due home tonight."

"What about our return match?"

"Which one? You haven't won a single game against me."

"You're not fair, Amin. You always take advantage of my bad days and score lots of points. But today, when I feel great, you back out."

I lean far back in my chair so I can stare at him properly. "You know what it is, my poor old Ezra? You don't have as much punch as you used to, and I hate myself for taking advantage of you."

"Don't bury me quite yet. Sooner or later, I'm going to shut you up once and for all."

"You don't need a racket for that. A simple suspension would do the trick."

He promises to think about it, brings a finger to his temple in a casual salute, and goes back to badgering the nurses in the corridors.

Once I'm alone, I try to go back to where I was before Ezra's intrusion and remember that I was about to call my wife. I pick up the phone, dial our number, and hang up again at the end of the seventh ring. My watch reads 1:12 P.M. If Sihem took the nine o'clock bus, she should have arrived home some time ago.

"You worry too much!" cries Dr. Kim Yehuda, surprising me by bursting into my cubbyhole. Continuing without pause, she says, "I knocked before I came in. You were lost in space. . . ."

"I'm sorry, I didn't hear you."

She dismisses my apology with a haughty hand, observes my furrowing brow, and asks, "Were you calling your house?"

"I can hide nothing from you."

"And, obviously, Sihem hasn't come home yet?"

Her insight irritates me, but I've learned to live with it. We've known each other since we were at the university together. We weren't in the same class—I was about three years ahead of her—but we hit it off right away. She was beautiful and spontaneous and far more open-minded than the other students, who had to bite their tongues a few times before they'd ask an Arab for a light, even if he was a brilliant student and a handsome lad to boot. Kim had an easy laugh and a generous heart. Our romance was brief and disconcertingly naïve. I suffered enormously when a young Russian god, freshly arrived from his Komsomol, came and stole her away from me. Good sport that I was, I didn't put up any fight. Later, I married Sihem, and then, without warning, very shortly after the Soviet empire fell apart, the Russian went back home; but we've remained excellent friends, Kim and I, and our close collaboration has forged a powerful bond between us.

"It's the end of the holiday today," she reminds me. "The roads are jammed. Have you tried to reach her at her grandmother's?"

"There's no telephone at the farm."

"Call her on her mobile phone."

"She forgot it at home again."

She spreads out her arms in resignation: "That's bad luck."

"For whom?"

She raises one magnificent eyebrow and shakes a warning finger at me. "The tragedy of certain well-intentioned people," she declares, "is that they don't have the courage of their commitments, and they fail to follow their ideas to their logical conclusion."

"The time is right," I say, rising from my chair. "The operation was very stressful, and we need to regain our strength. . . ."

Grabbing her by the elbow, I push her into the corridor. "Walk on ahead, my lovely. I want to see all the wonders you're pulling behind you."

"Would you dare repeat that in front of Sihem?"

"Only imbeciles never change their minds."

Kim's laughter lights up the hospital corridor like a garland of bright flowers in a home for the dying.

———

In the canteen, Ilan Ros joins us just as we're finishing our lunch. He sets his overloaded tray on the table and places himself on my right so that he's facing Kim. His jowls are scarlet, and he's wearing a loose apron over his Pantagruelian belly. He begins by gobbling up three slices of cold meat in quick succession and then wipes his mouth on a paper napkin. "Are you still looking for a second house?" he asks me amid a lot of voracious smacking.

"That depends on where it is."

"I think I've come up with something for you. Not far from Ashkelon. A pretty little villa with just what you need to tune out completely."

My wife and I have been looking for a small house on the seashore for more than a year. Sihem loves the sea. Every other weekend, my hospital duties permitting, we get into our car and head for the beach. We walk on the sand for a long time, and then we climb a dune and stare at the horizon until late in the night. Sunsets exercise a degree of fascination on Sihem that I've never been able to get to the bottom of.

"You think I can afford it?" I ask.

Ilan Ros utters a brief laugh, and his crimson neck shakes like gelatin. "Amin, you haven't put your hand in your pocket for so long that I figure you must have plenty socked away. Surely enough to make at least half of your dreams come true . . ."

Suddenly, a tremendous explosion shakes the walls of the canteen and sets the glasses tinkling. Everyone in the place looks at one another, puzzled, and then those close to the picture windows get up from their tables and peer out. Kim and I rush to the nearest window. Outside, the people at work in the hospital courtyard are standing still, with their faces turned toward the north. The facades of the buildings across the way prevent us from seeing farther.

"That's got to be a terrorist attack," someone says.

Kim and I run out into the corridor. A group of nurses is already coming up from the basement and racing toward the lobby. Judging from the force of the shock wave, I'd say the explosion couldn't have gone off very far away. A security guard switches on his transceiver to inquire about the situation. The person he's talking to doesn't know any more than he does. We storm the elevator, get out on the top floor, and hurry to the terrace overlooking the south wing of the building. A few curious people are already there, gazing out, with their hands shading their eyes. They're looking in the direction of a cloud of smoke rising about a dozen blocks from the hospital.

A security guard speaks into his radio: "It's coming from the direction of Hakirya," he says. "A bomb, maybe a suicide bomber. Or a booby-trapped vehicle. I have no information. All I can see is smoke coming from whatever the target was."

"We have to go back down," Kim tells me.

"You're right. We have to get ready to receive the first evacuees."

Ten minutes later, bits of information combine to evoke a veritable carnage. Some people say a bus was blown up; others say it was a restaurant. The hospital switchboard is practically smoking. We've got a red alert.

Ezra Benhaim orders the crisis-management team to stand by. Nurses and surgeons go to the emergency room, where stretchers and gurneys are arranged in a frenetic but orderly carousel. This isn't the first time that Tel Aviv's been shaken by a bomb, and after each experience our responders operate with increased efficiency. But an attack remains an attack. It wears you down. You manage it technically, not humanely. Turmoil and terror aren't compatible with sangfroid. When horror strikes, the heart is always its first target.

I reach the emergency room in my turn. Ezra's in command there, his face pallid, his mobile phone glued to his ear. With one hand, he tries to direct the preparations for surgical interventions.

"A suicide bomber blew himself up in a restaurant," he announces. "There are many dead and many more wounded. Evacuate wards three and four, and prepare to receive the first victims. The ambulances are on the way."

Kim, who's been in her office doing her own telephoning, catches up with me in ward five. This is where the most gravely wounded will be sent. Sometimes the operating room's too crowded, and surgery is performed on the spot.

Three other surgeons and I check the various pieces of equipment. Nurses are busy around the operating tables, making nimble, precise movements.

Kim proceeds to turn on the machines. As she does so, she informs me that there are at least eleven people dead.

Sirens are wailing outside. The first ambulances invade the hospital courtyard. I leave Kim with the machines and rejoin Ezra in the lobby. The cries of the wounded echo through the wards. A nearly naked woman, as enormous as her fright, twists around on a stretcher. The stretcher-bearers carrying her are having a hard time calming her down. She passes in front of me, with her hair standing up and her eyes bulging. Immediately behind her, a young boy arrives, covered with blood but still breathing. His face and arms are black, as though he's just come up out of a coal mine. I take hold of his gurney and wheel him to one side to keep the passage free. A nurse comes to help me.

"His hand is gone!" she cries.

"This is no time to lose your nerve," I tell her. "Put a tourniquet on him and take him to the operating room immediately. There's not a minute to spare."

"Very well, Doctor."

"Are you sure you'll be all right?"

"Don't worry about me, Doctor. I'll manage."

In the course of fifteen minutes, the lobby of the emergency room is transformed into a battlefield. No fewer than a hundred wounded people are packed into this space, the majority of them lying on the floor. All the gurneys are loaded with broken bodies, many horribly riddled with splinters and shards, some suffering from severe burns in several places. The whole hospital echoes with wailing and screaming. From time to time, a single cry pierces the din, underlining the death of a victim. One of them dies in my hands without giving me time to examine him. Kim informs me that the operating room is now completely full and that we have to start channeling the most serious cases to ward five. A wounded man demands to be treated immediately. His back is flayed from one end to the other, and part of one bare shoulder blade is showing. When he sees that no one is coming to his aid, he grabs a nurse by the hair. It takes three strapping young men to make him let go. A little farther on, another injured man, his body covered with cuts, screams and thrashes about madly, lunging so hard that he falls off his stretcher, which is wedged between two gurneys. He lies on the floor and slashes with his fists at the empty air. The nurse who's trying to care for him looks overwhelmed. Her eyes light up when she notices me.

"Oh, Dr. Amin. Hurry, hurry. . . ."

Suddenly, the injured man stiffens; his groans, his convulsions, his flailing all cease at once, his body grows still, and his arms fall across his chest, like a puppet whose strings have just been cut. In a split second, the expression of pain on his flushed features changes to a look of dementia, a mixture of cold rage and disgust. When I bend over him, he glowers at me menacingly, his teeth bared in a ferocious grimace. He pushes me away with a fierce thrust of his hand and mutters, "I don't want any Arab touching me. I'd rather croak."

I seize his wrist and force his arm down to his side. "Hold him tight," I tell the nurse. "I'm going to examine him."

"Don't touch me," the injured man says, trying to rise. "I forbid you to lay a hand on me."

He spits at me, but he's breathless, and his saliva lands on his chin, viscid and shimmering. Furious tears start spilling over his eyelids. I remove his jacket. His stomach is a spongy mass of pulped flesh that contracts whenever he makes an effort. He's lost a great deal of blood, and his cries only serve to intensify his hemorrhaging.

"He has to be operated on right away."

I signal to a male nurse to help me put the injured man back on his stretcher. Then, pushing aside the gurneys blocking our path, I make for the operating room. The patient stares at me, his hate-filled eyes on the point of rolling back into his head. He tries to protest, but his contortions have worn him out. Prostrate and helpless, he turns his head away so he won't have to look at me and surrenders to the drowsiness he can no longer resist.

2.

───────────

I leave the surgical unit around ten o'clock, long after dark.

I don't know how many people wound up on my operating table. Whenever I was finishing with one patient, another gurney would come through the swinging doors of the operating room. Some operations didn't require much time; others literally wore me out. I've got cramps everywhere and a tingling sensation in my joints. Every now and then, as I worked, my vision blurred and I had a spell of vertigo, but it wasn't until a kid nearly died on me that I decided to be reasonable and yield my place to a colleague. Kim, for her part, lost three patients, one after the other, as though she were under some evil spell that turned her efforts into dust. She was cursing herself as she left ward five. I think she went up to her office and cried her eyes out.

According to Ezra Benhaim, the tally of the dead has been revised upward and now stands at nineteen, among them eleven schoolchildren who were celebrating the birthday of one of their classmates in the fast-food restaurant where the bomb went off. We've performed four amputations, and thirty-three people have been admitted in critical condition. After receiving emergency treatment, about forty of the less seriously injured were picked up by relatives at the hospital; others went home under their own power.

In the hospital lobby, the relatives of patients still in our care bite their fingernails and pace around like sleepwalkers. Most of them don't seem to realize completely the enormity of the catastrophe that has just struck them. A frantic mother clings to my arm and pierces me with her eyes. "Doctor, how's my little girl? Is she going to make it?" A father turns up; his son's in intensive care. The father wants to know why the operation's lasting so long. "He's been in there for hours. What are you doing to him?" The nurses are being harassed in the same way. They defend themselves as best they can, calming people down and promising to get them the information they want. As I'm in the act of comforting an old man, an entire family spots me and presses in on me. I'm forced to beat a retreat to the outer courtyard and walk around the whole building in order to get back to my office.

Kim's not in hers. I go and ask Ilan Ros if he's seen her, but he hasn't. Nor have the nurses.

I change my clothes; I'm ready to go home.

In the parking lot, policemen are coming and going in a sort of hushed frenzy. The silence is filled with the crackling static of their radios. An officer gives instructions from in-

side a 4×4 with a light machine gun mounted on its dash-
board.

Exhilarated by the evening breeze, I reach my car. Kim's
Nissan is parked where it was when I arrived this morning,
its front windows rolled halfway down because of the heat.

When I leave the hospital grounds, the city seems calm.
The tragedy that has just shaken it can't make a dent in its
habits. Endless lines of vehicles are streaming toward the
Petach-Tikva expressway. The cafés and restaurants are
packed. Night people crowd the sidewalks. I take Gevirol to
Beit Sokolov, where a police checkpoint has been set up
since the attack. Drivers on this road are obliged to make a
detour around Hakirya, which draconian security measures
have now isolated from the rest of the city. I manage to
make my way to Hasmonaim Street, which is sunk in an
ethereal silence. From a distance, I can see the fast-food
restaurant the suicide bomber blew up. Officers from the
forensic police unit are combing the area, looking for clues
and taking samples. The front of the restaurant is completely destroyed; the roof of the whole south wing of the
building has fallen in. Blackish streaks bar the sidewalk. An
uprooted streetlight is lying across the roadway, which is littered with all sorts of debris. The violence of the blast must
have been unimaginable; the windows in the surrounding
buildings have been blown in, and the facades of some of
them are heavily damaged.

A cop comes from out of nowhere. "You can't stay
there," he tells me in a commanding voice.

He sweeps my car with his flashlight, lets it linger for a

while on my license plate, and then turns it on me. Instinctively, he takes a small step backward and puts his free hand on his pistol.

"Don't make any sudden moves," he warns me. "I want to see your hands on the steering wheel. What are you doing here? Can't you see this area's been sealed off?"

"I'm on my way home."

A second officer comes to the rescue. "How'd this guy get through?" he asks.

"Damned if I know," the first policeman says.

The second cop shines his own light on me, examining me with baleful, mistrustful eyes. "Your papers!"

I hand them to him. He checks them and points his light at my face again. My Arab name disturbs him. It's always like this after an attack. The cops are nervous, and suspicious faces exacerbate their predispositions.

"Get out and face the car," the first officer orders me.

I do what he says. He pushes me roughly against the roof of my vehicle, kicks my legs apart, and subjects me to a methodical search.

The other cop goes to have a look at what's inside my trunk.

"Where are you coming from?"

"From Ichilov Hospital. I'm Dr. Amin Jaafari. I'm a surgeon at Ichilov. I've just left the operating room. I'm exhausted, and I want to go home."

"Everything in order," the other policeman says, slamming the trunk lid closed. "Nothing to report in here."

His colleague refuses to let me go just like that. He moves

away a little and calls his headquarters to verify my employment status and the information on my driver's license and professional ID card. "He's an Arab, a naturalized Israeli citizen. He says he's just left the hospital, where he's a surgeon. . . . Jaafari, with two *a*'s. . . . Check with Ichilov. . . ." Five minutes later, he walks up to me, gives me my papers, and peremptorily orders me to return the way I came without looking back.

When I finally reach my house, it's nearly eleven o'clock. I'm drunk with fatigue and chagrin. I've been stopped by four police patrols along the way; each of them went over me and my car with a fine-toothed comb. It was no use showing my papers and announcing my profession; the cops had eyes only for my face. At one point, a young officer had enough of my protests and pointed his pistol at me, threatening to blow my brains out if I didn't shut my trap. His commanding officer had to intervene vigorously to put him in his place.

I'm relieved to be on my street again, safe and sound.

Sihem doesn't open the door for me. She hasn't come back from Kafr Kanna. The woman who cleans the house hasn't come, either. I find my bed unmade, just as I left it this morning. I check my answering machine: no messages. After such an agitated day as the one I've just spent, my wife's absence doesn't worry me inordinately. Every now and then she takes it into her head to prolong her visits to her grandmother. Sihem adores the farm. She likes to stay up late into the evening, atop a mound bathed by the tranquil light of the moon.

I go to my room to change my clothes and stop in front of the photograph of Sihem that reigns over my night table. Her smile is as big as a rainbow, but it isn't matched by the look in her eyes. Life hasn't always been kind to her. When she was eighteen, her mother died of cancer, and her father was killed in a road accident a few years later. It took forever before she finally agreed to accept me as her husband. She was afraid that fate, which had already been so cruel to her, would return and deal her another blow. After more than a decade of married life, despite the love I lavish on her, she still fears for her happiness, convinced that the smallest thing would be enough to shatter it forever. Nevertheless, luck continues to smile on us. When Sihem married me, my sole asset was an old asthmatic jalopy with a tendency to break down every few blocks. We set up house in a working-class suburb where the apartments had a lot in common with rabbit hutches. We had Formica furniture and not enough curtains for our windows. Now we've got a splendid residence in one of the most exclusive neighborhoods in Tel Aviv, and our bank account is fairly substantial. Every summer, we take off for some fantastic place. We know Paris, Frankfort, Barcelona, Miami, and several Caribbean islands, and we have loads of friends we're fond of and who are fond of us. We often entertain people in our home, and we're invited to many elegant parties. I've received several awards for my scientific research as well as for the quality of my work as a surgeon, and I've succeeded in building an excellent reputation in the region. Among our close friends and confidants, Sihem and I can count municipal dignitaries, civil and military authorities, and even a few stars of show business.

"You smile on me like luck, my dear," I say to her picture. "If only you could occasionally close your eyes."

I kiss my finger, lay it on Sihem's mouth, and hurry to the bathroom. I stand under a scalding shower for twenty minutes; then, wrapped in a robe, I go to the kitchen and nibble on a sandwich. After brushing my teeth, I go back to my bedroom, slip into my bed, and swallow a pill to ensure that I sleep the sleep of the just. . . .

The telephone resounds like a jackhammer in my brain, shaking me from head to foot, as though I've received an electric shock. Stunned, I grope around for the light switch, without success. The telephone keeps ringing, further confusing my perceptions. A glance at the alarm clock reveals that it's 3:20 in the morning. I extend my hand into the darkness again, uncertain whether I should concentrate on answering the phone or switching on the lamp.

I knock over something on the night table. Finally, after several tries, I grasp the receiver and pick it up.

The ensuing silence almost brings me to my senses.

"Hello?"

A man's voice says, "It's Navid."

It takes me a few moments to recognize the grating voice of Navid Ronnen, a senior police official. The sleeping pill I took continues to thwart my brain. I feel as though I'm slowly spinning around, suspended in a state somewhere between drowsiness and lethargy, dreaming a dream that scatters me through other inextricable dreams and ridiculously distorts Navid Ronnen's voice, which seems this evening to be arising out of a deep well.

I push back the covers and sit up. My blood throbs dully in my temples. I have to make a monumental effort to regain control of my breathing.

"Yes, Navid?"

"I'm calling from the hospital. We need you here."

In the semidarkness of the bedroom, the phosphorescent hands of the alarm clock twist around each other, leaving behind a greenish stain.

The telephone receiver feels like an anvil in my hand.

"I just got to bed, Navid. I operated on patients all day long, and I'm knocked out. Dr. Ilan Ros is on duty tonight. He's an excellent surgeon. . . ."

"I'm awfully sorry, Amin, but you have to come in. If you don't feel up to it, I'll send someone to get you."

"I don't think that will be necessary," I say, rummaging around in my hair.

I hear Navid clearing his throat on the other end of the line, hear that he's panting rather than breathing. I'm slowly regaining my wits and becoming aware of my surroundings.

Looking through the window, I watch a wispy cloud try to wrap up the moon. Higher up, thousands of stars gleam like fireflies. Not a sound or movement in the street. It's as though the city's been evacuated while I was sleeping.

"Amin?"

"Yes, Navid?"

"Don't drive too fast. We've got lots of time."

"Well, if it's not urgent, why—"

He interrupts me. "Please," he says. "I'm waiting for you."

"All right," I say, without trying too hard to understand. "But can you do me a little favor?"

"That depends."

"Inform your patrol cars and the people at your checkpoints that I'm coming through. Your guys seemed pretty nervous when I was driving home a little while ago."

"You still drive that white Ford?"

"Yes."

"I'll say a few words to them."

I hang up and lie still for a moment, staring at the telephone, intrigued by the nature of the call and Navid's impenetrable tone of voice. Then I put on my slippers and go to the bathroom to wash my face.

———

Two police cars and an ambulance are sending the beams from their rotating lights pivoting around the driveway to the emergency room. After the tumult of the day, the hospital has returned to its usual somber, morguelike state. Uniformed policemen are loitering here and there, some drawing nervously on the ends of cigarettes, others sitting in their vehicles and twiddling their thumbs. I park my car in the lot and head for the entrance. The night has cooled slightly, and a surreptitious breeze, contaminated by various sickly-sweet odors, is coming off the sea. I recognize Navid Ronnen's bulky silhouette as he stands on the steps. His right shoulder declines noticeably over his right leg, which a traffic accident shortened by an inch and a half ten years ago. I was the one who opposed amputation. At the time, I had just won my stripes as a surgeon, hands down, after a series of successful operations. Navid Ronnen was one of my most engaging patients. He had a steely courage and a persevering, though certainly questionable, sense of humor. The first nasty jokes I ever heard about the police came from him. Later, I operated on his mother, and that brought us even closer together. Since then, whenever he's got a colleague or a relative who needs surgery, he calls on me.

Dr. Ilan Ros is standing behind him, leaning in the doorway of the main entrance. The light from the lobby accentuates the coarseness of his profile. His hands in the pockets of lab coat and his belly hanging over his belt, he's staring absently at the ground.

Navid comes down the steps to meet me. He, too, has his hands in his pockets. His eyes avoid mine. I surmise from his attitude that dawn won't be breaking anytime soon. "Right," I say quickly, in an attempt to shake off the premonition that's starting to dog me. "I'll go up and change right away."

"Don't bother about that," Navid tells me in a toneless voice.

I've often seen him looking downcast when he's brought me a colleague on a stretcher, but the expression he's wearing tonight beats all the others for gloominess.

A light shiver grazes my back before extending its furtive crawl all the way into my chest.

"Has the patient died?" I ask.

Navid finally raises his eyes to me. I've seldom looked into unhappier ones.

"There's no patient, Amin."

"If that's the case, and there's no one to operate on, why have you dragged me out of bed at this hour?"

Navid doesn't appear to know where to start. His embarrassment infects Dr. Ros, who begins fidgeting in a most disagreeable way. I stare at the two of them, more and more irritated by the mystery they're keeping up in spite of their obvious mounting discomfort.

"Damn it, isn't anyone going to tell me what's going on?" I say.

With a thrust of his hips, Dr. Ros detaches himself from the wall he's been leaning against and returns to the reception desk, where two clearly desperate nurses pretend to stare at their computer screens.

Navid gathers his courage and asks, "Is Sihem at home?"

I feel my calves give way, but I recover quickly. "Why?"

"Is she at home or not, Amin?"

He's trying to sound insistent, but his eyes are panicking already.

An icy grip squeezes my guts. My Adam's apple sticks in my throat, preventing me from swallowing. "She's still at her grandmother's," I say. "In Kafr Kanna, near Nazareth. She went there to visit her family. . . . What are you getting at? What are you trying to tell me?"

Navid takes a step forward. The odor of his perspiration muddles me, intensifying the confusion I'm already feeling.

My friend doesn't know whether he should take me by the shoulders or keep his hands to himself.

"What the bloody hell is going on? Are you preparing me for the worst, or what? The bus Sihem was on . . . has there been an accident? Did the bus go off the road? Is that it? Is that what you're telling me?"

"It's not about the bus, Amin."

"Then what?"

"We've got a body on our hands and we've got to put a name on it," says a thickset, brutish-looking man who suddenly appears behind me.

I quickly turn back to Navid. "I think it's your wife, Amin," he concedes. "But to make a positive identification, we need you."

I feel myself disintegrating. . . .

Someone grabs me by the elbow to stop me from collapsing. In a fraction of a second, all my reference points have vanished. I no longer know where I am, don't even recognize the walls of the building where I've spent my whole professional career, all those years. . . . The hand at my elbow guides me into an evanescent corridor whose bright white lights slash my brain. I have a feeling that I'm walking on a cloud, that my feet are sinking into its surface. I step into the hospital morgue like a condemned man mounting the scaffold. A physician is standing at an altar. . . . The altar is covered with a bloodstained sheet. . . . Under the bloodstained sheet, obviously, there are human remains. . . .

I'm suddenly afraid of all the eyes turned in my direction. My prayers resound inside me like a subterranean echo.

The doctor gives me time to clear my head before reaching out a hand to the sheet. He keeps his eyes on the brute from a little while ago. At a signal from him, the doctor will pull back the sheet.

The policeman shakes his chin.

I cry out, "My God!"

I've seen mutilated bodies in my life. I've patched up dozens of them. I've seen some so badly damaged it was impossible to identify them. But the shredded limbs on the table in front of me pass all understanding. This is horror in its most absolute ugliness. . . . Only Sihem's head, strangely spared by the devastation that ravaged the rest of her body, emerges from the mass, the eyes closed, the mouth open a little, the features calm, as though liberated from their suffering. . . . I could think that she's peacefully sleeping, that she's going to open her eyes any minute and smile at me.

This time, my legs buckle, and neither the unknown person's hand nor Navid's can catch me before I fall.

3.

———————————

I've lost patients while I was operating on them. You never emerge completely unscathed from a failure like that. But the ordeal didn't stop there; I would then have to announce the terrible news to the relatives of the deceased, who were holding their breath in the waiting room. For as long as I live, I'll remember the anguished look they turned on me when I appeared before them after the operation. It was a look that was simultaneously intense and distant, fraught with hope and fear, and always the same, immense and profound as the silence that accompanied it. At that precise moment, I would lose confidence in myself. I'd be afraid of my words, of the shock they were going to cause. I'd wonder how the relatives were going to take the blow and what their first thoughts were going to be after they realized that the longed-for miracle had not taken place.

Today, it's my turn to *take the blow*. I believed that the sky was falling in on me when the doctor pulled away the sheet to reveal what was left of Sihem. Paradoxically, however, *my mind was blank.*

Now I'm slouched in a chair, and my mind is still blank. There's a vacuum in my head. I don't know if I'm in my office or someone else's. I see the diplomas hanging on the wall, the window with its blinds drawn, the shadows coming and going in the corridor, but it's as if all these things exist in a parallel world, into which I've been tossed without warning and without the least restraint.

I feel sickly, hallucinatory, devitalized. I'm nothing but a great heap of grief huddled under a lead blanket, incapable of telling whether I'm simply conscious of the misfortune I've been struck by or whether it's already annihilated me.

A nurse brought me a glass of water and withdrew on tiptoe. Navid hadn't stayed with me very long before his men came to fetch him. He followed them in silence, his chin buried in the hollow of his neck. Ilan Ros returned to his duties without once coming up to me and offering me his condolences. It was only much later that I realized I was alone in the office. Ezra Benhaim arrived ten minutes after my visit to the hospital morgue. He was on his last legs, visibly run-down and reeling from fatigue. He took me in his arms and held me very tightly. But there was an obstruction in his throat, and he could find no words to say to me. Then Ros came in and took him aside. I saw them conversing in the corridor. Ros kept whispering into his ear, and Ezra was having more and more trouble nodding his head. He had to lean against the wall in order to keep from falling down; I lost sight of him.

I hear vehicles in the drive and car doors slamming. Immediately, the sounds of footsteps resound in the corridors, accompanied by babbling voices and the occasional grunt. Two nurses hurry past, pushing a spectral gurney ahead of them. The shuffling footsteps invade the floor I'm on, fill the corridor, and draw nearer; some stern-looking men come to a stop in front of me. One of them, the one with short legs and a receding hairline, steps away from the group. It's the brute who complained about having a corpse on his hands and wanted me to help identify it.

"I'm Captain Moshé."

Navid Ronnen is there, standing two steps behind the captain. He isn't looking his best, my friend Navid. He seems overwhelmed, superseded. Despite his superior rank, he's suddenly been relegated to a secondary role.

The captain brandishes a document. "We have a search warrant, Dr. Jaafari."

"Search warrant?"

"You heard me. Please come with us—we're going to your house."

I try to read any possible glimmer in Navid's eyes; my friend stares at the ground.

I turn to the captain. "Why my house?"

The captain folds the document twice and slips it into the inside pocket of his jacket. "Our preliminary investigations indicate that the massive injuries sustained by your wife are typical of those found on the bodies of fundamentalist suicide bombers."

I can clearly make out the captain's words, but I can't

manage to attach any sense to them. Something seizes up in my mind, like a mollusk that abruptly closes its shell when it senses a threat from outside.

Navid offers an explanation: "It wasn't a planted bomb; it was a suicide attack. Everything suggests that the person who blew herself up in that restaurant was your wife, Amin."

The earth moves away under my feet. I do not, however, crumble. Rage props me up. Or maybe I'm just withdrawing. I refuse to hear one word more. I no longer recognize the world I live in.

————

The early risers hurry to the train stations and the bus shelters. Tel Aviv wakes up to itself, more obstinate than ever. However great the damage may be, no cataclysm is going to keep the world from turning.

Wedged between two brutes on the backseat of the police car, I look at the buildings filing past on one side and the other, and at the lighted windows where, for a few fleeting moments, figures appear like shadow puppets. The roar of a truck echoes down the street like the cry of a monster whose sleep has been disturbed; then the dazed silence of weekday mornings returns again. A drunk is flailing about in the middle of a square, probably trying to dislodge the lice that are eating him alive. At a red light, two law-enforcement officers are on the lookout, one eye in front, one eye behind, like chameleons.

Inside the car, everybody keeps quiet. The driver is at one
with his steering wheel. He's got broad shoulders and a
neck so short, it looks as though it's been pounded into his
body. Just once, our eyes meet in the rearview mirror, and a
chill runs down my spine. "Our preliminary investigations
indicate that the massive injuries sustained by your wife are
typical of those found on the bodies of fundamentalist suicide bombers." I have the feeling that these revelations will
haunt me for the rest of my days. They alternate in my mind,
slowly at first, and then, as if nourished by their excess,
they grow bolder and besiege me on all sides. The captain's
voice continues its hammering, clear and haughty, fully
cognizant of the extreme gravity of its declarations: "The
woman who blew herself up . . . the suicide bomber . . . it
was your wife. . . ." It swells, that loathsome voice; it surges
up like a dark wave, submerging my thoughts and shatter-
ing my incredulity before it suddenly withdraws, taking
with it entire sections of my being. I barely have time to see
my grief clearly before the groundswell rises again, throb-
bing, foaming, breaking over me as if driven raving mad by
my perplexity and determined to dismantle me, fiber by
fiber, until I fall apart. . . .

The cop on my right lowers the window. A stream of
fresh air lashes my face. The fetid smell of the sea reminds
me of rotten eggs.

Night is preparing to strike camp as the dawn grows impatient at the gates of the city. Through the spaces between
buildings, you can see the purulent stripes methodically fis-
suring the eastern horizon. It's a stricken night, deceived,

stunned, beating a retreat, encumbered with uncertainties and dead dreams. No trace of romance remains in the sky; no cloud proposes to temper the fiery zeal of the newborn sun. Even if its light were supposed to be Revelation itself, it would not warm my soul.

My neighborhood receives me coldly. A police patrol wagon is parked in front of my house. Police officers are standing on either side of my front gate. Another vehicle has been left half on the sidewalk with its red and blue lights still pirouetting. A few cigarettes glow in the blackness like an eruption of pimples.

They let me out of the car.

I push the gate, cross my yard, walk up the front steps, and open the door of my house. I'm clearheaded, but at the same time, I'm waiting to wake up.

The policemen know exactly what they have to do. They plunge through the foyer and hurry to the various rooms to begin their search.

Captain Moshé shows me to a sofa in the living room. "Can we have a little private talk, you and I?"

He guides me to my seat courteously but firmly. He applies himself to being worthy of his prerogatives; he cares a great deal about his status as a police officer, but his obsequiousness lacks credibility. He's nothing but a predator, sure of his tactics now that his prey is isolated. A bit like a cat playing with a mouse, he draws out his pleasure before devouring his meal.

"Please have a seat," he says.

He extracts a cigarette from a case, taps it against his

thumbnail, and screws it into the corner of his mouth. After applying a lighter to the cigarette, he blows the smoke in my direction. "I hope you don't mind if I smoke?"

He takes two or three more puffs, following the curls of smoke until they reach the ceiling and disperse.

"*She* really amazed you, didn't she?"

"Pardon me?"

"I'm sorry, I think you may still be in shock."

His eyes pass over the pictures hanging on the wall, inspect the corner shelves, slide across the imposing curtains, and make a few more stops here and there before turning their force back on me.

"How can a person give up such luxury?"

"Pardon me?"

"I'm thinking out loud," he says, shaking his cigarette in a sign of apology. "I'm trying to understand, but there are some things I'll never understand. It's so absurd, so stupid. . . . In your opinion, was there a chance of dissuading her? You surely knew all about her little project, didn't you?"

"What are you saying to me?"

"I believe I'm being quite clear. Don't look at me like that. You're not going to try to make me believe you didn't know anything, are you?"

"What are you talking about?"

"About your wife, Doctor. About the crime she committed yesterday afternoon."

"It wasn't her. It couldn't have been her."

"And why not? Why not her?"

I don't answer him; I limit myself to taking my head in my hands in an attempt to recover my wits. He stops me. With his free hand, he lifts my chin until he's staring straight into my eyes. "Are you a practicing Muslim, Dr. Jaafari?"

"No."

"And your wife?"

"No."

He furrows his brow. "No?"

"She didn't say her prayers, if that's what you mean by 'practicing.' "

"Strange . . ."

He rests one of his buttocks on the arm of the chair opposite me, crosses his legs, buries his elbow in his thigh, and grasps his chin delicately between his thumb and his index finger, squinting because of the smoke.

His murky gaze braces itself against mine.

"She didn't say her prayers?"

"No."

"Did she observe Ramadan?"

"Yes."

"Aha!"

He rubs the bridge of his nose without taking his eyes off me.

"A recalcitrant believer, in short—the image she needed so she could cover her tracks and work for the cause undisturbed. She was surely involved with a charitable organization or some such scam as that. They provide excellent cover, very easy to crawl under in case of problems. But behind all the volunteer work, there's always some high-profit business going on. The clever ones make some dough; the simpletons get promised a little corner in Paradise. I know a bit about all this—it's my job. I thought I'd seen the very depths of human stupidity, but I was kidding myself. I realize now that all I was doing was circling around the perimeter. . . ."

He blows some smoke in my face.

"She was friendly with the al-Aqsa Brigades, am I right? No, not al-Aqsa. We're told they don't give priority to suicide attacks. See, as far as I'm concerned, all these assholes are the same. Whether they're Islamic Jihad or Hamas, they're all part of the same pack of degenerates, ready to do anything to get a little publicity."

"My wife had nothing to do with those people. It's all a terrible misunderstanding."

"Well, here's a strange thing, Doctor. When we go and talk to the relatives of these nutcases after an attack, what they tell us is exactly what you just said. They give us the same stupefied look as the one on your face right now; events have taken them utterly by surprise. Is there a sort of general instruction to act like that in order to gain time? Or is it just a cheeky way of putting people on?"

"You're making a mistake, Captain."

He calms me with a gesture before returning to the charge.

"How did she seem yesterday morning when you left to go to work?"

"My wife went to visit her grandmother in Kafr Kanna three days ago."

"So you haven't seen her for the past three days?"

"No."

"But you've spoken on the telephone."

"No. She forgot her mobile phone at home, and there's no telephone at her grandmother's."

"Has she got a name, this grandmother?" he asked, taking out a little notebook from his inside pocket.

"Hanane Sheddad."

The captain writes it down.

"Did you drive her to Kafr Kanna?"

"No, she went by herself. I dropped her off at the bus terminal Wednesday morning. She took the eight-fifteen for Nazareth."

"You saw her leave?"

"Yes. I left the station at the same time her bus did."

Two policemen come back from my study carrying cardboard folders. A third is right behind them with my computer in his arms.

"They're taking away my files."

"We'll return them to you after we have a look at them."

"Those are confidential documents. They contain information about my patients."

"I'm very sorry, but we'll have to verify that for ourselves."

I hear a sequence of crashes and squeals in my house: doors slamming, drawers and furniture creaking.

"Let's go back to your wife for a moment, Dr. Jaafari."

"You're making a mistake, Captain. My wife has nothing to do with what you're accusing her of. She was in that restaurant exactly like any other customer. Sihem doesn't like to cook right after she comes back from a trip. She went there to have a bite to eat. It's as simple as that. I've shared her life and her secrets for fifteen years. I've learned to know her very well. If she was hiding something from me, I would have figured it out before long."

"I, too, was married to a beautiful woman, Dr. Jaafari. She was the pride of my life. It took me seven years to discover that she was hiding from me the most important information a man should have about his wife's fidelity."

"My wife had no reason to deceive me."

The captain looks for a place to dispose of his cigarette. I point out a little glass table behind him. He takes a last drag, longer than the preceding ones, and laboriously crushes out the butt in the ashtray.

"Dr. Jaafari, even a tried and tested man is never completely out of the woods. Life is a perpetual pain in the ass, a long tunnel mined with booby traps and covered with dog shit. When you're knocked down, it doesn't make much difference whether you jump back to your feet or stay on the ground. There's only one possible way of dealing with what you have to go through: You must prepare yourself every day and every night to expect the worst. Your wife didn't go into that restaurant to have a snack; she went there to have a blast. . . ."

"That's enough!" I yell, leaping to my feet in a fury. "One hour ago, I learned my wife had died in a restaurant targeted by a terrorist attack. Immediately afterward, you announce that she was the suicide bomber. That's far too much for an exhausted man to take. Let me cry for a while, then finish me off, but please, don't make me feel grief and horror at the same time."

"Please take your seat, Dr. Jaafari."

"Don't touch me. I forbid you to put your hands on me."

I push him away so aggressively that he almost falls over the little glass table behind him. He recovers quickly and tries to take control.

"Mr. Jaafari . . ."

"My wife had nothing to do with that massacre. It was a suicide attack, damn it! Not a housewives' quarrel. We're talking about *my wife*. Who's dead. Killed in that bloody restaurant. Like the others. With the others. I forbid you to soil her memory. She was a good woman, a very good woman. The complete opposite of what you're implying."

"A witness—"

"What witness? What does he remember, exactly? The bomb my wife was carrying, or her face? I shared my life with Sihem for more than fifteen years. I know her like the back of my hand. I know what she's capable of and what she's not capable of. Her hands were too white for the smallest stain to escape my notice. She's not your suspect just because her wounds are the worst, is she? If that's your only theory, there have to be others. My wife's wounds are the worst because she was the most exposed. The explosive device wasn't on her, but near her, probably hidden under her chair, or under the table she was sitting at. As far as I know, there's no official report that authorizes you to make such a serious accusation. Besides, a preliminary investigation is not necessarily the final word. Let's wait for the com-

munication from the terrorist commander. Some group will
have to claim responsibility for the attack. Maybe they'll
throw in some videocassettes, one addressed to your attention, others to the press. The suicide bomber, if there was
one, will be seen and heard."

"That's not necessarily the case with these morons.
Sometimes they make do with a fax or a telephone call."

"Not when it's a question of making a big impression.
And a female suicide bomber would cause a real sensation
in that line. Especially if she's a naturalized Israeli citizen
married to a prominent surgeon who's often been honored
by his city and who represents integration at its most successful. I don't want to hear any more of your filthy com-
ments about my wife, Captain, sir. My wife was a victim of
the attack; she wasn't the person who carried it out. I want
you to stop all this at once."

"*Sit down!*" the captain roars.

His outcry pierces me through and through.

My legs abandon me, and I sink down onto the sofa.

Drained of strength, I take my head in my hands and curl
up upon myself. I'm exhausted, worn down, wiped out; my
ship has a thousand leaks. Sleep manhandles me with unusual boorishness, but I refuse to go under. I don't want to
sleep. I'm afraid of nodding off and then waking up from
my dreams to the knowledge that the woman I cherished
most in the world is gone, that she died blown to bits in a
terrorist attack; afraid of having to suffer the same catastrophe, the same disaster, every time I wake up. . . . And
this captain who's in my face, why doesn't he crumble into

dust? I want him to disappear at once; I want the polter-geists that haunt my house to transform themselves into wind; I want a hurricane to smash my windows and carry me far away, far, far away from the doubt that's gnawing at my guts and mixing up my signs and filling my heart with awful uncertainties. . . .

4.

———————

Captain Moshé and his helpers keep me awake for twenty-four consecutive hours. They take turns, spelling one another in the squalid room where the interrogation takes place. This is a sort of rat hole with a low ceiling and dully painted walls. Above my head, there's a lightbulb inside a wire cage. The bulb produces a continuous sizzling sound that's just about to drive me mad. My sweat-soaked shirt is eating into my back with the voracity of a bunch of nettles. I'm hungry, I'm thirsty, I ache, and I don't see the end of the tunnel anywhere. They held me under the armpits and half-carried me to the toilets so I could piss. Before I could manage to undo my fly, I emptied half the contents of my bladder inside my underpants. A wave of nausea nearly caused me to smash my face against the toilet bowl. They literally dragged me back to my cell. Then the harassment began again, the questions, the fists striking the table, the little slaps to prevent me from turning my eyes aside.

Every time sleep distorts my judgment, they shake me from head to foot and turn me over to the zealous attentions of another officer, someone well rested and fresh as a daisy. The questions are always the same. They resound in my head like muffled incantations.

I sway in the metal chair that's flaying my behind and grab the table to keep from falling over backward; then, suddenly, I let everything go like a disjointed puppet, and my face hits the edge of the table violently. I believe I've split open an eyebrow.

"The bus driver has formally identified your wife, Doctor. He recognized her photograph at once. He said she did indeed get on the eight-fifteen bus for Nazareth last Wednesday morning. But as the bus reached the outskirts of Tel Aviv, less than twenty kilometers from the terminal, she asked to be let off. She claimed it was an emergency. The driver was obliged to stop on the shoulder of the road. Before he pulled away, he saw your wife climb into a car that had been following the bus. That's the detail that caught his attention. He didn't get the car's license number, but he says it was an older-model Mercedes, cream-colored. Does that description mean anything to you, Dr. Jaafari?"

"What should it mean to me? I've got a late-model Ford, and it's white. My wife had no reason to get off that bus. Your driver's talking nonsense."

"If that's the case, he's not alone. We sent someone to Kafr Kanna. Hanane Sheddad says she hasn't seen her granddaughter for more than nine months."

"She's an old woman. . . ."

"Her nephew, who lives on the farm with her, says the same thing. Therefore, Dr. Jaafari, if your wife hadn't set foot in Kafr Kanna for more than nine months, where did she spend those last three days?"

Where did she spend those last three days? Where did she go? Where was she? An unfathomable murmur drowns out the police officer's words; I don't hear them anymore. I see only his eyebrows, twitching according to the traps he lays for me, his mouth, going over some arguments to which I am by now impervious, and his hands, describing his impatience, or, rather, his determination. . . .

Another officer shows up, his face concealed behind dark glasses. He waves a peremptory finger at me as he talks. His threats fizzle out in the shallow waters of my clearheadedness. He doesn't stay long and goes away muttering curses.

I don't know what time it is, or even whether it's day or night. They took my watch away. And my questioners take care to remove theirs before they enter my room.

Captain Moshé comes to see me again, empty-handed. The search of my house has yielded nothing. He's exhausted, too. He stinks like a crushed cigarette butt. His features are drawn and his eyes are red, he hasn't shaved for a couple of days, and his mouth has a tendency to go slack on one side.

"All the evidence inclines us to believe that your wife did not leave Tel Aviv, not on Wednesday nor on any of the following days."

"That's not enough to make her a criminal."

"Your marital relations were—"

I cut him off. "My wife didn't have a lover."

"If she had one, she was under no obligation to inform you of the fact."

"We had no secrets from each other."

"Real secrets aren't shared."

"There's surely an explanation, Captain. But not the one you think you've found."

"Be reasonable for a second, Doctor. If your wife lied to you, if she made you believe she was going to Nazareth and then sneaked back into Tel Aviv as soon as your back was turned, that means she wasn't playing fair with you."

"You're the one who's not playing fair, Captain. You tell lies to get to the truth. But your bluff isn't going to work. You can keep me awake every day and every night, and you still won't make me say what you want to hear. You'll have to find some other donkey to pin this tail on."

He gets upset and steps into the hall. Comes back a little later with a stiff forehead and jaws like frozen pulleys. His breath submerges me. He's on the verge of cracking up.

When he scratches his cheeks, his fingernails make a frightful rasping sound.

"I simply refuse to swallow this story. How can you say you didn't notice anything unusual in your wife's behavior recently? Were you two living under the same roof or not?"

"My wife was no Islamist. How many times do I have to say that? You're making a mistake. Let me go home. I haven't slept for two days."

"Neither have I, and I have no intention of closing my

eyes before I get to the bottom of this. The forensic team is adamant: Your wife was killed by the explosive charge she was carrying. A witness who was sitting at an outside table and was only slightly injured swears he saw a pregnant woman in the part of the restaurant where some schoolkids had organized a party to celebrate the birthday of one of their little classmates. He recognized this woman in a photograph, without hesitation. And it was your wife. Now, you've declared that she wasn't pregnant. Your neighbors don't remember having seen her pregnant at any time during your residence in the neighborhood. And the autopsy report is adamant on this point, too: no pregnancy. So what was it that made your wife's belly so big? What did she have under her dress, if not the goddamned bomb that took the lives of seventeen people, including a bunch of kids who were just having a good time?"

"Wait for the videocassette. . . ."

"There won't be a videocassette. And to tell you the truth, I couldn't possibly care less about cassettes. They're not my problem. My problem is something else, and it's making me sick. I absolutely have to know how a beautiful, intelligent, modern woman, esteemed by the people around her, thoroughly assimilated, pampered by her husband, and worshiped by her friends—the majority of whom are Jews—how such a woman could get up one day and load herself with explosives and go to a public place and do something that calls into question all the trust the state of Israel has placed in the Arabs it has welcomed as citizens. Do you realize the gravity of this situation, Dr. Jaafari? We expect a certain amount of treachery, but not of this nature. I've picked over everything I could find out about the pair of you: your connections, your habits, your little weaknesses. The result? I'm totally stumped. I'm a Jew and an officer in the Israeli armed services, and yet I haven't received a third of the considerations this city handed out to you two on a daily basis. And that fact shakes me up so much, I can't believe it."

"Don't try to take advantage of my physical and mental state, Captain. My wife is innocent. She had absolutely nothing to do with any fundamentalists. She never met any, never spoke to any, never had dreams about any. My wife went into that restaurant to have lunch. *Lunch*. Nothing more, and nothing less . . . Now leave me alone. I'm wiped out."

Whereupon I cross my arms on the table, lay my head on them, and fall asleep.

———

Captain Moshé comes back again and again. At the end of the third day, he opens the door of the rat hole and shows me the corridor. "You're free to go, Doctor. You can go home and take up a normal life again, if possible. . . ."

I collect my jacket and stagger along a corridor where some officers with their coats off, their shirtsleeves rolled up, and their ties undone observe me in silence. They look like a pack of wolves watching their prey get away when they'd been sure it was trapped. At a window, a clerk with a rugged profile gives me back my watch, my key ring, and my wallet and has me sign a release; then, with a short, sharp movement, he snaps down the little pane of glass that separates us. Someone escorts me to the exit. Daylight assails me as soon as I set foot outside the building. It's a fine day; an enormous sun is shining down on the city. The noise of traffic brings me back to the land of the living. I stand still on the steps for a few moments, gazing at the vehicles in their everyday ballet, the dancing punctuated now and then by the sound of horns. The streets aren't crowded. The neighborhood looks neglected. The trees that line the roadway don't seem to be very happy about it, and the pedestrians loitering about are as sad as their shadows.

At the bottom of the steps, there's a large automobile with its engine running. Navid Ronnen is at the wheel. He puts one foot on the ground and an elbow on the car door and waits for me to join him. I understand at once that he's had something to do with my liberation.

When I get close to him, he frowns. Because of my swollen eye.

"They beat you?"

"I slipped."

He's not convinced. "It's the truth," I tell him.

He doesn't insist. "Shall I drop you off at your house?"

"I don't know."

"You're in a pitiful state. You need a shower, a change of clothes, and something to eat."

"Have the terrorists sent the cassette?"

"What cassette?"

"The videocassette for the attack. Have you finally found out who the suicide bomber was?"

"Amin . . ."

I back up to avoid his hand. I can't bear to have another person lay a hand on me, not even by way of comfort.

My eyes lock onto Navid's eyes and don't let go.

"Since they've released me, it means they're certain my wife had nothing to do with the bomb."

"I have to take you home, Amin. You need to recover your strength. That's the important thing right now."

"If they let me go, Navid, come on . . . if they let me go, that means they've . . . What have they found out, Navid?"

"They've found out that *you*, Amin, that *you* had nothing to do with the bomb."

"Only me?"

"Only you."

"And Sihem?"

"You have to pay the *knass*. That's the rule."

"A fine? And since when is that rule in effect?"

"Ever since the fundamentalist suicide bombers—"

I interrupt him by waving a finger. "Sihem isn't a suicide bomber, Navid. Try to remember that. Because it's the most important thing in the world to me. My wife isn't a child-killer. Have I made myself understood?"

I leave him standing there and go away without knowing where. I don't want a ride home anymore; I no longer need someone to put a hand on my shoulder; I don't want to see anyone, not anyone on my side, not anyone on the other side.

Night surprises me on a stone slab facing the sea. I haven't the least notion of what I did with my day. I believe I fell asleep somewhere. My three days and three nights of captivity have left me completely unraveled. I've lost my jacket. I must have left it on a public bench, or maybe someone stole it from me. I've got a large stain on the upper part of my pants, and splashes of vomit splotch my shirt; I've also got a vague memory of puking under a footbridge. How did I dawdle my way to this stone slab overlooking the sea? I don't know.

Away out on the water, an ocean liner twinkles.

Closer in, the waves hurl themselves desperately against the rocks. Their racket resounds in my head like the blows of a club.

The sea breeze refreshes me. I gather myself around my legs, sink my chin between my knees, and listen to the sounds of the sea. My eyes gradually grow blurry; my sobs overtake me, jostling together in my throat and setting off a series of shivers that pass through my body in every direction. I take my face in my hands and groan and groan until finally I begin shouting like a man possessed into the deafening roar of the waves.

5.

Someone has attached a poster to the iron gate of my house. It's not exactly a poster—it's the front page of a daily newspaper with a large circulation. Above an imposing photograph depicting the bloody chaos in and around the restaurant targeted by the terrorists, there's a headline in large print, spread across three columns: THE FILTHY BEAST IS AMONG US.

The street's deserted. An anemic streetlamp sheds its light, a pallid halo that hardly extends beyond the lamp itself. My neighbor across the street has his curtains drawn. It's barely ten o'clock in the evening, and there's no light in any window.

Captain Moshé's vandals didn't hold themselves back. My study has been turned upside down. The same disorder reigns in the bedroom: the mattress flipped over, the sheets on the floor, the bedside tables and dresser violated, the drawers spilled out onto the carpet. My wife's lingerie lies among the slippers and cosmetic products. They took down my pictures to see what was behind them. Someone even trod on an old family photograph.

I have neither the strength nor the nerve to go to the other rooms and inspect the damage.

The mirror on the armoire shows me my reflection. I don't recognize myself. Disheveled, wild-eyed, hollow-cheeked, unshaven, I look like a madman.

I undress and go to the bathroom to fill the tub; on the way, I find some food in the fridge and pounce on it like a famished beast. I eat standing up, using my dirty hands, nearly choking on the big mouthfuls I gulp down in quick succession with pathetic voracity. I empty a basket of fruit and two platefuls of cold meat, drain two bottles of beer—one long pull apiece—and lick the dripping sauce off each of my ten fingers, one by one.

I have to pass in front of the mirror again before I realize I'm completely naked. I don't remember wandering around the house in my birthday suit since before I got married. Sihem was a stickler for certain principles.

Sihem . . .

How far away it is already, all that!

I slip into the tub; the water warms me to my core. I close my eyes and try to dissolve myself in the hot torpor washing over me. . . .

———

"My God!"

Kim Yehuda's standing in my bathroom, incredulous. She looks to the right, then looks to the left; she claps her hands together as if she can't admit what she's seeing. With a quick about-face, she opens the little cupboard on the wall and reaches in, looking for a towel.

"You spent the night in there?" she cries, simultaneously horrified and outraged. "What were you thinking, damn it? You could have drowned!"

It's hard for me to open my eyes. Maybe because of the daylight. I slowly become aware that I've slept in the bathtub all night. The water's gone cold, and my limbs don't react; they've become hard as wood. My thighs and my forearms are purple. I also notice that I can't stop my body from trembling or my teeth from chattering.

"Amin, what are you trying to do to yourself? Stand up and get out of there this minute. *I'm* going to catch my death just from looking at you."

She helps me out of the tub, wraps me in a bathrobe, and rubs me vigorously from my head to my calves.

"I can't believe it," she keeps saying. "How could you fall asleep in water up to your neck? Don't you even realize? I had a premonition this morning. Something told me I absolutely had to pass this way before I went back to the hospital. . . . Navid called me right after they let you go. I came by three times yesterday, but you hadn't come home yet. I figured you went and stayed at some relative or friend's house."

She leads me to my room, puts the mattress back on the bed, and lays me down on it. My limbs shiver harder and harder, and my jawbones are about to crack. "I'm going to fix you something warm to drink," she says, spreading a blanket over me.

I hear her busying herself in the kitchen. She calls out a few questions about where this or that is. My mouth is trembling too uncontrollably for me to articulate a word. I curl up under the blanket in a fetal position, making myself very small so my body can warm up a little.

Kim brings me a large bowl of tisane, lifts my head, and sets about pouring the scalding, sweetened beverage into my mouth. A burning flood spreads through my chest and moves into my stomach.

I'm quivering so much that Kim has trouble holding me.

She puts the bowl down on the bedside table, adjusts my pillow, and helps me lie down again. "When did you get home? Late last night, or early this morning? I found the gate unlatched and the front door wide open—I was afraid something terrible had happened to you. Anyone could have come into your house."

I can't think of anything to say to her.

She explains to me that she has to perform an operation before noon. She tries to reach the housekeeper in order to ask her to show up, but she keeps getting her answering machine. Finally, she leaves a message. Kim's uneasy about abandoning me, unsupervised, to my own devices; she tries in vain to come up with a solution. When she takes my temperature, she calms down, and then, after fixing me a meal, she tells me good-bye, promising to return as soon as she can.

I didn't see her leave.

I think I went back to sleep. . . .

———

The screeching of a gate wakes me up. I throw off the covers and go to the window. Two teenagers are skulking around on my property with stacks of paper under their arms. My lawn is covered with dozens of photographs cut from newspapers. Some gawkers have gathered across the street. I yell, "Go away!" but I can't open the window, so I rush to the door and out into the yard. The two teenagers clear off in a hurry. Barefoot, my head boiling, I pursue them into the street.

"Dirty terrorist! Piece of shit! Arab traitor!"

The invective stops me short. Too late—I'm right in the middle of an overexcited mob. Two bearded men with plaited hair spit on me. I'm pushed about. "Is that how your people say thank you, dirty Arab? By biting the hand that pulled you out of the shit?" Some shadowy figures slip behind me to cut off any possibility of retreat. A jet of saliva strikes my face. A hand pulls me by the collar of my bathrobe. "Look at the house you live in, you son of a bitch. What more do you have to have before you learn to say thanks?" They push and shake me. "We'll have to disinfect this prick before we finish him off." A kick in the belly bends me in half; another kick straightens me up. My nose is split open, and then my lips. My arms aren't enough to protect me. A shower of blows rains down on me, and the earth shifts under my feet.

————

Kim finds me lying in the middle of the driveway. My attackers chased me into the yard and kept punching and kicking me long after they knocked me to the ground. Their bulging eyes and frothing mouths made me think they were going to lynch me.

Not a single neighbor came to my aid; no charitable soul had sufficient presence of mind to call the police.

Kim says, "I'm going to take you to the hospital."

"No, not the hospital. I don't want to go back there."

"I think you've got something broken."

"Please don't insist. Please don't."

"In any case, you can't stay here. They'll kill you."

Kim manages to get me back to my room. She helps me dress, throws a few things into a bag for me, and inserts me into her car.

The bearded guys with the plaited hair appear out of nowhere, probably alerted by a lookout.

"Let him croak," one of them says to Kim. "He's just a piece of shit."

Kim's tires squeal as she pulls away.

We speed through the neighborhood like a runaway racing car in a minefield.

———

Kim drives directly to an outpatient clinic near Yafo. The X rays show no fractures, but evidence of extensive trauma is now visible on my right wrist and knee. A nurse disinfects the cuts on my arms, sponges off the blood caked on my split lips, cleans my battered nostrils. She thinks I'm suffering from the consequences of a drunken brawl; her gestures are full of commiseration.

I leave the room hopping on one foot, with a heavy bandage around my right hand.

Kim offers me her shoulder. I prefer to lean on the wall.

She takes me to her place, a loft on Sderot Yerushalayim that she bought back when she was living with Boris. Sihem and I used to come here often to celebrate some happy event or just to spend a pleasant evening with friends. The two women got along very well, even though mine was rather reserved and remained constantly on her guard. Kim didn't care—she loved to have guests and throw parties. And ever since getting over Boris's defection, she's redoubled her hostessing efforts.

We take the elevator. An old granny rides up with us to the third floor. On the fifth-floor landing, a dejected puppy waits, with one end of his leash closed in the far door. The puppy belongs to Kim's neighbor, who, if she follows her common practice, will get rid of it as soon as it reaches maturity and get herself another one.

Kim has trouble with the lock, as she does whenever she's nervous. She grimaces in frustration, and dimples form in her cheeks. Her flush of anger looks good on her. Finally, she finds the right key and steps aside to let me enter.

"Make yourself at home," she says.

She takes off my jacket and hangs it in the entrance hall. With a movement of her chin, she directs me to the living room, where a wicker chair and a worn old leather armchair are staring daggers at each other. Half the wall is taken up by a large surrealist painting, which rather looks like the doodles of unstable children fascinated by blood-

red and coal-black. There's a wrought-iron pedestal table
that Kim discovered in a flea market where she loves to go
on weekends. On this table, along with some terra-cotta
bric-a-brac and an ashtray as full as an urn, there's one
of our leading newspapers—open to a photograph of my
wife.

Kim lunges for it, but I hold her back by one hand. "It
doesn't matter," I say.

Confused, she nevertheless gathers up the newspaper
and throws it into a wastebasket.

I sit in the armchair, near some French windows that
open onto a balcony covered with flowerpots. The apartment offers an unencumbered view of the avenue. The traffic is intense. The evening is settling in, and the night
promises to be feverish.

We have dinner in the kitchen, Kim and I. She picks
at her food; I chew mine without conviction. The newspaper photograph is stuck to my eyeballs. A hundred
times, I feel the urge to ask Kim what she thinks about
this news story, which the journalists are embellishing in
accordance with their various obsessions; a hundred times,
I feel the urge to take her chin in both my hands, stare
straight into her eyes, and insist that she tell me truth-
fully whether, in her soul and conscience, she believes
that my wife, Sihem Jaafari, the woman with whom she
shared so many things, was capable of strapping a load of
explosives onto herself and going to detonate them in
the midst of a party. But I don't dare take advantage of
Kim's solicitude for me. At the same time, in my heart of

hearts, I pray that she won't say anything either, that she won't take my hand in a gesture of compassion; one consideration too many, and I may not survive. We're fine together, just like this: Our silence protects us from ourselves.

She clears the table without making very much noise and offers me a cup of coffee. I ask her for a cigarette. She frowns. I stopped smoking years ago.

"You're sure that's what you want?"

I don't answer her.

She holds out her pack, followed by her lighter. The first puffs set off sparks in my brain. The following puffs make me dizzy.

"Would you mind dimming the lights?"

She switches off the ceiling light and turns on a lamp. The relative darkness of the room soothes my anxieties somewhat. Two hours later, we're in the same position, seated facing each other, our eyes lost in our thoughts.

"We have to go to bed," she announces. "I'm half-asleep, and I've got a busy day tomorrow."

She puts me in the guest room. "Is everything all right? You don't need more pillows?"

"Good night, Kim."

She takes a shower and then turns off the light in her room.

Later, she comes into my room to see if I'm asleep. I feign unconsciousness.

———

A week has passed, and I still haven't gone back to my house. Kim's harboring me, taking care not to upset my delicate balance. A technician probing a bomb could hardly be more cautious.

My wounds have scarred over, my contusions gone down, and my bashed knee no longer obliges me to hop about, but my wrist is still wrapped in a bandage.

When Kim's not here, I shut myself up in my room and I don't move. Go out? Where would I go? The street holds no attractions for me. There wasn't anything for me out there yesterday, and there's surely even less today. It's useless to try to return to my old life and my familiar objects when my heart's not in it. Here in this room, with the curtains drawn, I feel protected. Here, I don't run many risks. I'm not completely comfortable, but I'm not suffering any injuries, either. Still, I have to make my way back up the slope. The bottom's no good for anybody. In this kind of implosion, if you don't react very quickly, you lose control of absolutely everything. You become a spectator of your own collapse, and you don't realize that the abyss is about to close over you forever.

One evening, Kim suggested we go to visit her grandfather in his beach house. I said I wasn't ready to renew contact with anyone or anything that wouldn't ever again be the same as it was before. I need to get some distance, let time pass, figure out what's happening to me. And yet, I generally cloister myself in my room all day long and think of nothing at all. Otherwise, I install myself near the French windows and spend most of my time looking at the vehicles wiggle along the avenue. I don't really see them. Just once, I consider the idea of getting behind the steering wheel and driving in some randomly chosen direction until my radiator bursts, but I have neither the nerve nor the energy to go back to the hospital and pick up my car.

As soon as I was able to walk without supporting myself on the nearest wall, I asked to see Navid Ronnen. I want to give my wife a decent burial. I can't stand to imagine her so cramped, shut up in that refrigerated drawer in the morgue with a label attached to her toe. In order to spare me a bout of futile anger, Navid brings me the proper forms, duly filled out; all he needs is my signature.

I pay the fine and collect my wife's body without saying anything to anyone. I'm determined to bury Sihem in the strictest privacy. I want her grave to be in Tel Aviv, the city where we met for the first time and where we decided to live until death should us part. Except for the grave digger and the imam, I'm alone at the cemetery.

When the hole where the best part of my life will rest from now on is entirely covered with earth, I start feeling a little better. It's as if I've performed a task that had previously seemed inconceivable. I listen to the imam reciting verses from the Qur'an until he's finished, and then I slip some banknotes into his hand—which he pretends to withdraw at first—and set out for Kim's loft on foot.

On my way, I walk down a broad esplanade that overlooks the sea. Tourists take photographs and wave at one another. Some amorous young couples put their heads together in the shade of the trees; others walk hand in hand along the jetty. I go into a small café, order a cup of coffee, take a seat in a corner near the picture window, and calmly smoke one cigarette after another.

The sun begins to lower its profile. I hail a taxi and ask to be dropped off on Sderot Yerushalayim.

Kim has guests. No one hears me come in. I can't see the living room from the entrance hall. I recognize Ezra Benhaim's voice, then Navid's much heavier bass, and then the liquid tones of Kim's older brother Benjamin.

Ezra clears his throat and says, "I don't see the connection."

"There's always a connection where you don't suspect one," says Benjamin, who taught philosophy at Tel Aviv University for a long time before joining a very controversial pacifist movement in Jerusalem. "That's the mistake we keep on making."

"Let's not exaggerate," Ezra protests politely.

"We've got dueling funeral processions coming from both sides. Can we call that progress?"

"The Palestinians refuse to listen to reason."

"Maybe we refuse to listen to them."

"Benjamin's right," Navid says in a calm, inspired voice. "The Palestinian fundamentalists send kids to blow themselves up in bus shelters. As soon as we collect our dead, our leaders send up the copters to smoke a few Arab hovels. Then, just when the government is getting ready to declare victory, a fresh attack sets the clock back. How long can it go on?"

At this precise moment, Kim comes out of the kitchen and discovers me in the hall. I put a finger on my lips, imploring her not to give me away, then turn on my heels and head for the landing. Kim tries to catch up with me, but I'm already in the street.

6.

———————

And here I am, back in my neighborhood—like a ghost returning to the scene of the crime. I don't know how I wound up here. After fleeing from Kim's, I chose an avenue at random and walked until I got thigh cramps. Then I took a bus to the terminal, ate dinner in a little restaurant in Shapira, and roamed from one square to another before discovering that my feet had carried me to the part of the city where Sihem and I chose to live seven years ago, when we were certain that our home would be an ineradicable shrine to our love for each other. It's a handsome, quiet neighborhood, jealously guarding its posh mansions and its tranquillity. Here the owners of Tel Aviv's great fortunes take their ease, along with a colony of parvenus, among them some Russian immigrants recognizable by their uncouth accents and their maniacal efforts to impress their neighbors. The first time we passed this way, Sihem and I, we were immediately captivated by the area. Daylight seemed much brighter here than elsewhere. We loved the carved stone facades, the wrought-iron gates, and the aura of felicity around the houses, with their wide-eyed windows and their lovely balconies. At the time, we were living in an incongruous suburban neighborhood, in a little apartment on the fourth floor of an unremarkable building where loud domestic quarrels were the order of the day. We were keeping strictly to a tight budget in order to put aside enough money to move, but we were far from imagining that we'd ever unpack our bags in such an exclusive part of town. I'll never forget Sihem's joy when I took the blindfold off her eyes and showed her *our* house. She jumped so high off her seat in the car that her head cracked the cover of the interior light. She was as happy as a little girl whose dearest birthday wish comes true, and seeing her like that utterly enchanted me. How many times did she grab me by the neck and kiss me on the mouth, in plain view of any nosy onlookers, she who would blush red as a beet whenever I dared to give her a public squeeze? She pushed the gate open and made a beeline for the heavy oaken front door. She was so impatient that she made it hard for me to find the right key. I can still hear her cries of joy echoing in my head. I see her again, spinning around with her arms flung out in the middle of the dining room, like a ballerina intoxicated by the dance. I had to put my arms around her to restrain her exuberance. Her eyes flooded me with gratitude; her happiness stunned me. And there, in the huge bare room, we spread out my overcoat on the marble floor and made love like two teenagers,

dazzled and frightened at once by their bodies' first ec-
stasy. . . .

It must be eleven o'clock or maybe a little earlier, and
there's not a soul in sight. The street of my triumphs is deep
asleep; its lamps are distressingly dull. Deprived of its romance, my house looks like a haunted place—there's something terrifying about the darkness it's wrapped in. You'd
think it had been abandoned for generations. We neglected
to close the shutters, and some windows are broken. Pieces
of paper litter the lawn and lie among the garden's withered
flowers. In our flight the other day, Kim forgot to lock the
gate; malicious visitors have swung it wide open and left it
that way, and now it's making a low clanking sound, pierc-
ing the silence like a diabolical complaint. The lock has
been literally gutted with an iron bar. They've also ripped
one of the gate's hinges out of the ground and wrecked the
doorbell cover. The newspaper cuttings attached to my wall
as signs of public condemnation flap in the breeze among
some heinous graffiti. A lot has happened while I've been
away.

There's mail in my mailbox. A little envelope among the
bills attracts my attention. No return address, just a stamp
and a postmark. The envelope was mailed from Bethlehem.
My heart nearly jumps out of my chest when I recognize Sihem's handwriting. I run into the bedroom, turn on the
lights, and sit down near the bedside table, where the photograph of my wife has pride of place.

Suddenly, I freeze.

Why Bethlehem? What news is it bringing me, this letter

from beyond the grave? My fingers tremble and I begin a series of dry-throated gulps. For a moment, I think about
waiting until later to open the envelope. I don't feel up to
turning the other cheek or adding to the sum of the misfortune that's been following me around like a dog ever since
the attack. The tornado that knocked down all my sup-
ports has left me terribly fragile; I wouldn't have the
strength to live through another dirty trick—and at the
same time, I don't feel capable of waiting a second longer.
All my fibers are stretched to the breaking point; my exposed nerves are on the verge of shorting out completely. I
take a deep breath and rip open the envelope. I could slit
my wrists and feel less threatened, less endangered, than I
do now. Prickly sweat runs down my back. My heart beats
faster and faster, resounding dully in my temples and filling
the room with giddy echoes.

The letter is short, without any date or salutation. Barely
five lines, hastily scribbled on a piece of paper torn from a
school notebook.

> *What use is happiness when it's not shared,*
> *Amin, my love? My joys faded away every time*
> *yours didn't follow. You wanted children. I*
> *wanted to deserve them. No child is completely*
> *safe if it has no country. Don't hate me.*
>   *Sihem*

The sheet of paper gets away from me, falls from my
hands. With one blow, everything collapses. The woman I

married for better or worse, *forever*, the woman who pulled me through my most difficult years, the woman who hung my projects with shimmering garlands and filled my soul with her sweet presence—I can't find that woman anywhere. Nothing of her remains, not on me, not in my memories. I snatch the frame that holds her captive, now irredeemably out of date, and turn it around; I can't reconcile myself to its image of what I used to think was the best thing that ever happened to me. It's as though I've been catapulted over a cliff and sucked into a bottomless abyss. I shake my head, *no*; I shake my hands, *no*; I shake my whole being, *no*. I think, I'm going to wake up. But I'm awake. I'm not dreaming. The letter lies at my feet, exceedingly real, calling the totality of my convictions into question, pulverizing one by one all my most rock-ribbed certitudes. My last reference points have hit the fucking road. *It's not fair*. The movie of my three-day captivity replays in my mind. Captain Moshé's voice returns to persecute me; its hollow cries conjure up inextricably swirling images. A bright flash occasionally lights up one or another of them: I see Navid waiting for me at the bottom of the steps, Kim picking me up in pieces from my driveway, my attackers trying to lynch me in my own yard. I put my hands on my head and abandon myself to the growing, stupefying weariness inside me.

What the hell is this supposed to mean, Sihem, my love?

You think you know. Then you lower your guard and act as though everything's just great. With the passage of time, you stop paying as much attention to things as you should.

You're confident. What more can you do? Life is smiling on you. So is luck. You love and are loved. You can afford your dreams. Everything's fine, everything blesses you. . . . and then, without warning, the sky falls in on your head. And once you're flat on your back, you realize that your life, your *whole* life—with its ups and downs, its pains and pleasures, its promises and failures—hangs and has always hung by a thread as flimsy and imperceptible as the threads in a spider's web. Suddenly, the slightest sound terrifies you, and you no longer feel like believing in anything whatsoever. All you want to do is close your eyes and think no more.

———

"You forgot to close your door again!" Kim scolds me.

She's standing in the bedroom doorway with her arms folded over her chest. I didn't hear her come in.

"Why did you leave tonight? Navid and Ezra came over just to see you. What's the matter, can't you bear the sight of your friends anymore?"

Her smile grows confused and fades away.

"Say, what's up? You look really strange."

My appearance is sufficiently substandard to cause her to lunge at me, grab my wrists, and examine them to make sure they're unharmed. "You haven't cut yourself, have you? Man! You don't have a drop of blood in your face. Have you seen a ghost, or what? What's wrong? Say something, damn it! You took some shit, is that it? Look in my eyes and tell

me whether you took some shit. It's crazy, what you're doing to yourself, Amin!" she shouts, all the while looking
around for the poison capsule or the bottle of sleeping pills.
"I can't leave you alone for one minute!"

I watch her get on her knees and look under the bed, feeling around here and there.

I don't recognize my voice when I blurt it out to her: "*It
was her,* Kim! My God! How could she?"

Kim stops all words and gestures, draws herself up but
remains on her knees. She doesn't understand. "What are
you talking about?"

She spots the letter at my feet, grabs it, reads it. Her
brow furrows gradually, notch by notch, as she reads. "God
Almighty!" She sighs.

She looks me up and down, unsure how to behave. An
awkward moment ensues, and then she spreads her arms. I
nestle against her, making myself very small, and for the
second time in fewer than ten days, I begin bawling like a
whole pack of babies, me, who hadn't shed a single tear
since Grandfather died, more than thirty years ago.

————

Kim stays with me until morning. When I awaken, I find her
curled up in an armchair near my bed, visibly exhausted.
Sleep surprised us when we least expected it. I don't know
which of us went down first. I passed out with my shoes on
my feet and my jacket zipped up to my throat. Curiously, I
feel as though a great storm has passed. Sihem's photo-

graph on the bedside table touches nothing in me. Her smile has faded; her eyes have rolled up into her head. My grief has crushed me without finishing me off.

Outside, a few twittering birds fray the morning silence. It's over, I tell myself. The sun's coming up, on the street and in my mind.

Kim takes me to visit her grandfather, who lives in a little house at the seashore. Old Yehuda hasn't been informed about my troubles, and so much the better, as far as I'm concerned. I need people to look at me the way they always have done. If they fall silent, I don't want to attribute that to embarrassment; if they smile, I don't want to take that as a sign of pity.

During the drive, Kim and I avoid talking about the letter. To keep from running any risks, we keep silent. Kim's in the driver's seat of her Nissan, looking through her sunglasses. Her hair flutters in the wind of our passage. She looks straight ahead and keeps a tight grip on the steering wheel. For my part, I contemplate my bandaged wrist and try to take an interest in the purring of the engine.

Old Yehuda welcomes us with his habitual courtesy. His wife died a generation ago, and his children have all gone to other lands to live their lives. He's recovering from a bout of prostate cancer that shriveled him in the course of a few months and left him an emaciated old man with bony cheekbones and immobile eyes in a ravaged face. Still, he's always happy to receive visitors. For him, it's like being brought back to life. He lives like a hermit in spite of himself, forgotten inside the house he built with his own hands, in the midst of books and photographs depicting, in great detail, the horrors of the Shoah. So when a relative or friend comes and knocks on his door, it's as if someone were lifting the trapdoor of his underground lair to let a little light shine into his night.

The three of us have lunch in a restaurant close to the beach. It's a beautiful day. Except for a ruffled cloud that's dissolving into thin air, the sun has the sky to itself. A few families are on the sand: Some lounge around an improvised picnic; others walk along the shoreline in water up to their calves. Children chase one another, chirping like birds.

"Why didn't you bring Sihem with you?" old Yehuda asks me point-blank.

My heart stops beating.

Kim, likewise taken by surprise, nearly chokes on an olive. She'd been afraid her grandfather would come out with something like this, but she'd expected it to happen much sooner, and when it didn't, she relaxed her vigilance. I see her stiffen as her face goes crimson, and she waits for my response like a guilty man awaiting his sentence. I wipe my lips, and at the end of a meditative silence, I reply that Sihem was unavoidably detained. Old Yehuda nods and goes back to stirring his soup. I realize that he was just making small talk, probably to break the silence that had quarantined each of us in his own corner.

After the meal, old Yehuda goes back home for his siesta and Kim and I leave to take a walk in the sand. We patrol the beach from one end to the other, our hands behind our backs, our heads elsewhere. From time to time, a bold wave rolls up to us, licks our ankles, and surreptitiously with-draws.

Exhausted and recharged at the same time, we climb a dune to watch the sunset. The night shields us from the dis-order of things. That does us good, both of us.

Yehuda comes and gets us. We have dinner on his ve-randa, listening to the sea tearing at the rocks. Every time the old man starts to tell us the story of his family, victims of the German concentration camps, Kim reminds him that he's promised not to spoil the evening. He acknowl-edges that he has indeed agreed not to trot out the mis-eries of yesteryear once again and then sinks back into his chair, a little miffed at having to keep his memories to himself.

Kim suggests I sleep on the cot in the upstairs room; she takes the foam mattress on the floor. It's still early when we turn out the lights.

All night long, I try to understand *how* Sihem arrived at the point she reached. What was the moment when she started to get away from me? How could I have failed to no-tice anything? Surely, she tried to give me some sign, to tell me something I wasn't quick enough to catch. What was I thinking? It's true, her eyes had lost a great deal of their brilliance recently, and she laughed less and less; but was *that* the message I had to decipher, the outstretched hand I absolutely had to grasp in order to prevent the flood from sweeping her away from me? Pretty pathetic clues for some-one who spared no effort to give each kiss its celebration and every embrace its orgasm. I turn my memories over from top to bottom in search of a detail that might soothe my soul, but I find nothing conclusive. Between Sihem and me, there was a perfect love, a harmonious serenade that seemed unmarred by a single false note. We didn't talk; we *told* ourselves, the way a storyteller tells a romantic idyll. Had she ever uttered a groan, I would have taken it for singing, for I couldn't suspect that she was on the periphery of my happiness when she embodied it utterly. Only once did she speak of dying. We were on the shore of a Swiss lake, gazing on a sunset that turned the horizon into a work of art. "I wouldn't survive you by as much as a minute," she confided to me. "You're all the world to me. Whenever I can't see you, I die a little." She was radiant that evening, Sihem was, in her white dress. The men seated at the tables around us devoured her with their eyes. As though inspired by her freshness, the lake welcomed the freshness of the night. . . . No, she wasn't warning me then, not in that place; she was so happy, so attentive to the soft breeze ruffling the surface of the lake; she was the most beautiful gift life could offer me.

———

Old Yehuda gets up first. I hear him making coffee. I push away the covers and put on my trousers and my shoes, and then I step over Kim, who's lying curled up at the foot of my bed with the sheet twisted around her legs.

Outside, the night's packing up.

I go downstairs to the kitchen, where Yehuda's sitting at

the table with his hands around a bowl of steaming coffee. "Good morning," I say.

"Good morning, Amin. There's coffee on the stove."

"Later," I tell him. "First I want to see the sunrise."

"An excellent idea."

I go down a little path to the beach, sit on a rock, and concentrate on the infinitesimal crack that's starting to appear in the darkness. The breeze rummages around under my shirt and tousles my hair. I wrap my arms around my knees, delicately place my chin on them, and stare unwaveringly at the opalescent streaks gently lifting the horizon's coattails. . . .

"Let the sound of the waves drown out all that racket inside you," old Yehuda says, surprising me as he eases himself down to sit at my side. "It's the best way to clear your mind of thoughts."

He listens to a wave gargling in the hollow of the rock, wipes his nose with his fist, and speaks in a confiding tone: "One should always look at the sea. It's a mirror that can't lie. Among other things, looking at it has taught me to stop looking behind me. Before, every time I looked over my shoulder, I found my old sorrows and my old ghosts, still intact. They were preventing me from regaining my taste for living. Do you understand what I mean? They were spoiling my chances of rising from my ashes."

He digs up a pebble and holds it distractedly, as though weighing it.

"That's the reason why I chose to spend my last years here and die in my house on the seashore. A man who looks at the sea turns his back on the misfortunes of the world. Somehow, he resigns himself to them."

His arm describes an arc when he flings the stone into the waves.

"I spent the better part of my life tracking down past suffering," he says. "As far as I was concerned, nothing could beat a remembrance ceremony or a memorial dedication. I was convinced that the only reason I'd survived the Holocaust was to keep its memory alive. All I wanted to look at was gravestones. Whenever I heard that a big one was being unveiled somewhere, I'd jump on a plane at once so I could get a seat in one of the rows in front. I recorded all the conferences that dealt with the Jewish genocide and traveled the world from one end to the other so I could recount what our people endured in the concentration camps, suspended between the gas chambers and the crematory ovens. And yet, personally, I didn't see much of the Holocaust. I was four years old. I occasionally wonder whether some of my memories aren't really the result of traumatic experiences I had well after the war, in dark theaters where they showed documentaries about the Nazi atrocities."

After a long silence, during which he has to struggle to control his emotions, he goes on. "I was born to be happy. Providence seemed to have stacked all the cards in my favor. I was sound in body and mind. My family was well-off. My father was a physician in Berlin's most prestigious clinic. My mother taught art history at the university. We lived in a splendid house in a fashionable neighborhood—with a yard like a big meadow. I was the youngest of six children, and we had servants who attended to my every need.

"In the city, it was obvious that things weren't exactly rosy. Racial discrimination was gaining ground—every day there was a little more. People made disagreeable remarks when they passed us in the street. But as soon as we got back to our house, we were in the very bosom of happiness.

"Then one morning, we had to give up our tranquil haven and join the cohorts of the innumerable, confused families who'd been driven from their homes and delivered up to the demons of Kristallnacht. Some mornings are just more night. And that long night in the fall of 1938 was certainly the blackest. I'll always remember those people, their empty eyes, the yellow stars that so clashed with the cut of their clothes, and, especially, the silence that accompanied their misfortune."

"The yellow star made its first appearance in September 1941."

"I know. However, there it is, pinned to each of my memories, deeply entrenched in every corner of my brain. I wonder if I wasn't born with it. I was only knee-high, but it seems to me I could see above the adults' heads without ever catching even a glimpse of the horizon. It was a most unusual morning, totally gray. Grayness surrounded us, and the mist erased our tracks on the road of no return. I remember every tremor in the stricken faces around me. I remember their fraught stupor; I remember how they smelled of carrion. When one of the damned became too exhausted to go on and a blow from a rifle butt stretched him out on

the ground, I raised my eyes to my father, trying to understand; he rooted around in my hair and whispered, 'It's
nothing. Everything will be all right. . . .' I swear to you,
right now, as I'm speaking to you, I feel his fingers against
my skull, and they give me gooseflesh. . . ."

"Sabba," Kim says, joining us and admonishing her
grandfather.

The old man lifts his arms like a little rascal caught with
his finger in the jam jar. "I beg your pardon," he says. "It's
stronger than I am. It does no good for me to promise not
to probe the old wounds anymore. That's exactly what I do,
whenever I think I have something to say."

"That's because you don't look at the sea enough, Sabba,
dear," Kim tells him, gently massaging his neck.

Old Yehuda considers his granddaughter's words as
though he were hearing them for the first time. His eyes
cloud over, become dim and distant, haunted by tragic evo-
cations. For a few moments, he seems not to know where he
is, and it's only with difficulty that he snaps out of his daze.
Then, with his granddaughter's hands supporting his neck,
he recovers a little of his lucidity.

"You're right, Kim. I talk too much," he says, and then,
in a quavering voice: "I'll never understand why the survivors of a tragedy feel compelled to make people believe
they're more to be pitied than the ones who didn't make it."

His gaze runs over the sand on the beach, dives into the
midst of the waves, and gets lost in the open sea, while his
diaphanous hand moves slowly up to touch his granddaughter's.

The three of us, each paralyzed in his own silence, contemplate the horizon, which the dawn lights up with a thousand fires; and each of us knows for certain that the rising sun of this day, like all those that have gone before it, will be incapable of bringing sufficient light into the hearts of men.

———————

7

Eventually, Kim took it upon herself to go and pick up my car at the hospital. She also brought back the latest news, which is that I'm persona non grata over there. Ilan Ros has succeeded in uniting the majority of the medical personnel against me. Some of the people who signed petitions opposing my return even suggested that I should be stripped of my Israeli citizenship.

I don't find Ilan Ros's attitude particularly surprising. About ten years ago, he lost his younger brother, a sergeant with the border guards, in an ambush in southern Lebanon. He's never been able to get over that. Although in the course of things he and I are often together, he never lets himself forget where I come from and what I am. In his eyes, despite my talents as a surgeon and my aptitude for getting on with people professionally as well as socially, I'm still the Arab: inseparable from the wog handyman and, to a lesser degree, from the potential enemy. In the beginning, I suspected him of flirting with some separationist movement; I was mistaken. He was simply jealous of my success. I didn't hold it against him, but he wouldn't be appeased. When my work was recognized and praised, he attributed my honors to a simple demagogic measure designed to advance the cause of the societal integration of which I was the most convincing specimen. The suicide attack in Hakirya came at just the right moment to justify the stirrings of his old demons.

"Look at you. Alone and talking to yourself," Kim says, surprising me.

Her freshness surprises me, too. She looks like a fairy arising from a fountain of youth, with her black hair cascading down her back and her big eyes, emphasized by black eyeliner. She's wearing flawlessly tailored white pants and a light blouse perfectly wedded to the voluptuous contours of her chest. Her face is serene and her smile radiant. I have the feeling that I'm noticing her at last, after all these many days and nights I've spent with her in a sort of trance. As recently as yesterday, she was only a shadow hovering around my introspections. I'm unable to remember how she was dressed or if she was wearing makeup or whether her hair was spread out on her shoulders or pinned up in a chignon.

"One is never really alone, Kim."

She pushes a chair close to me and straddles it backward. Her perfume nearly intoxicates me. I see her translucent hands grow white around the joints when she grasps the back of the chair. Her mouth trembles and hesitates when she asks, "So who were you talking to?"

"I wasn't talking; I was thinking out loud."

The calmness of my tone emboldens her. She leans over the back of the chair to get a closer look at me and speaks in what's supposed to be a confiding tone: "Well, in any case, you looked as though you were in good company. Sad, but somehow handsomer."

"It was probably my father. I've been thinking about him a lot recently."

She takes my hands to comfort me. Our eyes meet but turn aside at once, fearful of discovering a gleam that might upset them.

"How's your wrist?" she asks, by way of dispersing the awkward air that has suddenly settled over the room.

"It keeps me awake. My hand, too. It feels like there's a little stone planted in the middle of my palm, and I've got a tingling sensation in the joints."

Kim lightly touches the bandage on my hand and gently moves my fingers. "In my opinion, we ought to go back to the clinic and find out for sure what's going on. The first X ray wasn't good. You might have a fracture."

"I tried to drive this morning. I had trouble with the steering wheel."

This news flusters her. She asks, "Where did you want to go?"

"I have no idea."

She stands up, frowning. "Let's go see about your wrist," she says. "That seems more reasonable."

She drives me back to the clinic in her car. During the trip, she says not a word, no doubt preoccupied with trying to guess where I wanted to go this morning when I got behind my steering wheel. She must be wondering whether all the precautions she takes on my behalf are stifling me.

I'm dying to put my hand on hers as a sign of how lucky I feel to have her at my side, but no matter where I look, I can't find the strength that would make such a gesture possible. I'm afraid that she'll take her hand away, that the words won't come, that my clumsiness may botch up my honorable intentions—I think I'm losing confidence in myself.

A fat nurse takes charge of me. She dislikes my appearance at first sight and in a peremptory tone suggests that I should change my diet in favor of grilled steaks and raw vegetables, because, she whispers in my ear, I look like someone on a hunger strike. The physician examines my first X ray, declares it perfectly legible, and balks for a while before consenting to x-ray me a second time. The new picture confirms the preceding diagnosis: no detectable fracture, no crack of any kind, just a huge trauma at the base of my index finger and another, less extensive one centered on my wrist. He prescribes an ointment, some anti-inflammatory pills, and some pills to help me sleep, and then he sends me back to the nurse.

As we leave the clinic, I catch sight of Navid Ronnen. He's sitting in an automobile in the medical building's parking lot, one foot propped on the open door, his hands behind his head, patiently staring at the top of the streetlight.

"Is he tailing me, or what?" I say, surprised to find him here.

"Don't be a dummy," Kim scolds me, offended by the question. "He called me on my mobile phone, asking for news of you, and I told him to meet us here."

I realize how boorish my question was; I don't apologize.

"Don't let your grief spoil your good manners, Amin."

"What are you talking about?" I ask her testily.

"It's no use being disagreeable," she replies, looking un-flinchingly into my eyes.

Navid gets out of his car. He's wearing a tracksuit stamped with the colors of the national soccer team, a pair of new running shoes, and a black beret. His endless aero-bics classes and workout sessions, which he puts himself through with religious rigor, don't seem capable of revers-ing his increasingly burdensome corpulence. Navid's not proud of this bearish bulk, which magnifies the difficulties of his shortened leg and turns his gait into an awkward shuffle, thus compromising the seriousness and authority he'd like to project.

"I was jogging nearby," he declares, as though trying to justify himself.

"There's no law against that," I retort.

I realize as I speak that my allusion's aggressive and out of place, but, strangely enough, I don't feel any need to soften it. You might even say I'm deriving a certain amount of pleasure from my surly attitude, a pleasure as dark as the shadow covering my soul. I don't recognize this gratuitous nastiness of mine, nor do I see how I can control it.

Kim pinches my underarm, a gesture that doesn't es-cape Navid. "Well," he growls, deeply disappointed, "if I'm bothering you . . ."

"Why would you say such a thing?" I exclaim, trying to redeem myself.

He gives me a withering look, so forceful, it makes his facial muscles quiver. My question gets to him more than my pathetic allusion. He comes closer and stares at me in a way that prevents my eyes from turning aside. He's very angry.

"You're asking *me* that, Amin?" he says in a furious voice. "Am *I* the one who's avoiding *you*? Isn't it you who skulks away every time you think I might be anywhere around? What's wrong with you? Have I done you some wrong without realizing it, or are you just acting like an asshole?"

"It's not that at all. I'm glad to see you."

He squints at me. "That's strange, because it's not what I read in your eyes."

"But it's the truth."

"Suppose we go have a drink," Kim suggests. "On me. You pick the place, Navid."

Navid agrees to forget about my boorish behavior, but he's still hurt. He takes a deep breath, looks over his shoulder to ponder his choice, and then proposes Chez Zion, a quiet little bar not far from the clinic, where they serve the best cocktail snacks around.

While Kim follows Navid's car, I try to pinpoint the reasons for my aggressiveness toward a person who stood by me when others were systematically making me an object of public contempt. Is it because of what he represents, because of his cop's badge? If so, I must admit, it can't be easy for a cop to continue to be friends with the husband of a suicide bomber. I build up theories and then tear them down, hoping I won't let myself go too far, hoping to refrain from considerations that could strip me bare and isolate me more completely in my torment. Curiously, at the same moment when I resolve to guard against losing control, I feel an irrepressible (and, it seems to me, appropriate) urge to be offensive. Is it my refusal to dissociate myself from Sihem's offense that's pushing me toward hostility? If so, then what am I becoming? What am I trying to prove, or to justify? And what do we really know about what's just and what isn't? There are the things that suit us; there are the things that don't. Whether we're right or wrong, we lack discernment in equal measure. That's how men live: When they're at their worst, they do their best, and when they're at their best, it doesn't mean very much. . . . My thoughts drive me into a corner; they make light of my qualms, feed on my fragility, exploit my grief. I'm aware of how they're sapping me and I let them do it anyway, like an overconfident watchman abandoning himself to drowsiness. My tears may well have drowned a little of my sorrow, but my rage is still there, like a tumor buried deep inside me, or like a monster of the abyss, crouched in the darkness of its lair, waiting for the right moment to rise to the surface and terrify its world. Kim can feel it, too. She knows I'm trying to externalize the horror wallowing around in my guts; she sees that my aggressiveness is only a symptom of the extreme violence laboriously welling up in me, waiting to gather together the propelling charges of its eruption. If she doesn't want me out of her sight for a second, it's because she hopes to limit the damage. But my inexplicable conduct stymies her; she's beginning to doubt.

We take a table on the terrace of the little café, which sits in the middle of a paved square. There are other customers around us, some in good company, others alone, staring pensively at their glass or cup. The café's proprietor is a tall, strapping fellow with an unruly mane blending into his Viking's beard. He's blond as a bale of hay, his arms covered with hair from his wrists to his shoulders. He looks as though he's suffocating under his sailor's shirt. He comes to our table to say hello to Navid, whom he apparently knows, then takes our order and withdraws.

When Navid sees me pull out a pack of cigarettes, he asks, "You smoke? Since when?"

"Ever since my dreams went up in smoke."

My reply causes Kim some consternation, but she limits herself to clenching her fists. Navid considers it calmly, his lower lip drawn down. For a moment, I think he's just about to put me in my place, but then he leans back in his chair and folds his hands on the mound of his belly.

The proprietor returns with a tray and serves Navid a frothy beer, Kim a glass of tomato juice, and me a cup of coffee. He says something agreeably amusing to the police commander and again withdraws. Kim's the first to pick up her drink and takes three quick sips in a row. She's quite disappointed in me, and she's keeping quiet to avoid blowing up in my face.

"How's Margaret?" I ask Navid.

He doesn't answer right away. On his guard, he gives himself the time to take a swallow of his beer before risking a reply. "She's fine, thanks."

"And the children?"

"You know how they are. Sometimes they get along; sometimes they're not talking to one another."

"You're still thinking about marrying Edeet to that mechanic?"

"She's the one who wants it. He's her choice."

"You think he's a good match for her?"

"In such matters, you don't think; you pray."

I nod. "You're right. Marriage is always a gamble. It obeys its own logic. Making calculations or taking precautions is useless."

Navid sees that my words aren't hiding any traps. He relaxes a little, savors a mouthful of beer, smacks his lips, and gives me a look of immense consideration. "And your wrist?" he says.

"A nasty bruise, but nothing broken."

Kim fishes a cigarette out of my pack. I hold out my lighter to her. She leans forward, draws on the cigarette voraciously, and sits back up, exhaling a great cloud through her nostrils.

"How's the investigation going?" I ask straight out.

Kim chokes on a half-inhaled mouthful of smoke.

Navid, once again on his guard, stares at me intensely.

"I don't want to argue with you, Amin."

"I don't want to argue, either. I just have a right to know."

"Know what, exactly? What you refuse to accept?"

"Not anymore. *I know it was her.*"

Kim puts her face quite close to mine and gazes at me,

squinting through the smoke from the cigarette in the corner of her mouth; she can't see what I'm getting at.

Navid gently pushes away his beer mug, as if clearing the surrounding area so he can have me all to himself. "You know *what* was her?"

"I know it was her who blew herself up in that restaurant."

"You do? Since when?"

"Is this an interrogation, Navid?"

"Not necessarily."

"In that case, why not just tell me how the investigation's going?"

Navid lets himself fall against the back of his chair. "We're at a standstill. Spinning our wheels."

"What about the old cream-colored Mercedes?"

"My father-in-law has one like that."

"With all the tools you've got, with all your networks of snitches, you still haven't—"

"It's not a question of tools or snitches, Amin," he says, interrupting me. "What we're dealing with is a woman who was above all suspicion, a woman who hid her tracks so completely that our best investigator, our supersleuth, keeps running into the same impasse no matter what trail he follows. But in cases of this nature, it's reassuring to realize that all we need is a clue, a single clue, and the machine will start purring again. Do you think you have such a clue?"

"I don't think so."

Navid wiggles around in his chair—heavily—puts his elbows on the table, and reaches for the beer mug he pushed aside a minute ago. He runs his finger around the edge of the glass, wiping away flecks of foam. An implacable silence settles over the terrace.

"At least you know who the suicide bomber was," Navid says. "That's a step forward."

"How about me?"

"You?"

"Yes, me. Have I been cleared, or am I still a suspect?"

"You wouldn't be here sipping your coffee if anyone could blame you for anything, Amin."

"So why did I get beaten up in front of my own house?"

"That didn't have anything to do with the police. That was an angry mob, and anger's like marriage: It doesn't always obey its own logic. You could have filed a complaint, but you didn't."

I stub out my cigarette in the ashtray, light another one, and find its taste suddenly disgusting. "Tell me, Navid," I say. "You've seen a lot of criminals, both repentant and unrepentant, and a lot of plain psychopaths, too. How can a person, just like that—how can a person just strap on a load of explosives and go blow herself up in the middle of a party?"

Visibly uncomfortable, Navid shrugs his shoulders. "That's what I ask myself every night. I can never even make sense of the question, much less come up with an answer."

"Have you ever met any of . . . these people?"

"Plenty."

"So how do they explain what they've done? How do they explain their lunacy?"

"They don't explain it. They accept it."

"You can't imagine what it does to me to think about those cases. How the hell is it possible for an ordinary human being, sound in body and mind, to make that choice? Does he have a fantasy or a hallucination that convinces him he's been given a divine mission? How can he give up his plans, his dreams, his ambitions, and decide to die an atrocious death in the midst of the worst kind of barbarism?"

I believe tears of rage cloud my vision at the same rate as my words choke and splutter in my throat. Kim agitates her thighs feverishly under the table. By now, her cigarette's just a twig of ashes suspended in the air.

Navid sighs, giving himself time to choose his words. He perceives the pain I'm in, and it seems to cause him to suffer, too.

"What can I tell you, Amin? I think even the most seasoned terrorists really have no idea what has happened to them. And it can happen to anyone. Something clicks somewhere in their subconscious, and they're off. Their motives aren't all equally solid, but generally, whatever it is, it comes over them like that," he says, snapping his fingers. "Either it falls on your head like a roof tile or it attaches itself to your insides like a tapeworm. Afterward, you no longer see the world in the same way. You've got only one thing on your mind: the thing that has taken you over, body and soul. You want to lift it so you can see what's under it.

And from that point on, you can never turn back. Besides, you're no longer giving the orders. You think you're in control, doing what you want to do, but it's not true. You've nothing but the instrument of your own frustrations. For you, death and life come down to the same thing. Somewhere, you must have renounced everything that could have given you a chance of returning to earth, to the real world. You float. You hover. You're an extraterrestrial. You live in a kind of limbo, stalking houris and unicorns. As for this world, you don't even want to hear about it anymore. You're just waiting for the right moment to cross the threshold. The only way to get back what you've lost or to fix what you've screwed up—in other words, the only way to make something of your life—is to end it with a flourish: turn yourself into a giant firecracker in the middle of a school bus, or launch yourself like a torpedo against an enemy tank. Ka-boom! The big bang, with a special bonus prize—full martyr status. The way you see it, the day of your funeral procession will be the day when you're exalted in other people's eyes. The rest—the day before, the day after—that's not your problem; as far as you're concerned, it doesn't exist."

"Sihem was so happy," I remind him.

"That's what we all thought. Apparently, we were all wrong."

We stay at that café until late in the night. Our evening out allows me to let off steam and get rid of the stale thoughts polluting my mind. My aggressiveness dissipates as our conversation evokes more and more memories. Several times, I'm surprised to feel my eyes brimming with tears, but I stop them from going any farther. Every time my voice starts to crack, Kim's hand seeks out mine to comfort me. Navid's very patient. He puts up with my dis-courtesies and promises to keep me informed of the inves-tigation's progress. By the time we say good night, we're reconciled, bonded more closely than ever before.

Kim drives me back to her house. We eat sandwiches in the kitchen, chain-smoke in the living room, talk at length about everything and nothing, and then go to our rooms. A little later, Kim comes in to see if I need anything. Before turning out the light, she asks me point-blank why I didn't say anything to Navid about the letter.

I spread out my arms and confess: "I have no idea."

8.

——————————

According to Kim, the Ministry of Health has received an enormous amount of mail from my former patients and their relatives, in whose opinion I'm as much a victim as those who died in the restaurant my wife blew up. The hospital is divided; passions have cooled a bit, and a good many of my detractors are wondering if the petitions they signed were reasonable. Given the complexity of the situation, the hospital hierarchy has asserted that my case is beyond its purview and declared its readiness to accept the decision of higher authorities.

As for me, my decision is taken: I'm not going back to my office, not even to collect my personal belongings. The cabal that Ilan Ros led against me has had a profound effect on my outlook. The thing is, I've never paraded my religious heritage anywhere. Ever since I left the university, I've tried to carry out my civic duties scrupulously. All too aware of the stereotypes that mark me out in the public square, I strive to overcome them, one by one, by doing the best I can do and putting up with the incivilities of my Jewish comrades. When I was still young, I realized that sitting between two chairs made no sense; I had to choose a side, and fast. I chose to be on the side of my ability, and I made my convictions my allies. With these, I was sure, I'd eventually force people to respect me. I don't think I ever, not even once, broke the rules I set for myself. Those rules were like Ariadne's thread for me, except it was sharp as a razor blade. For an Arab who stood out from the rest—and who gave himself the satisfaction of graduating first in his class—the least mistake could have been fatal. Especially when he was the son of a Bedouin, stumbling under the weight of the prejudices his ancestry entailed. I lugged the caricature of that ancestry around with me like a convict's ball and chain; it frequently exposed me to general human meanness, sometimes turned me into an object; at other times, it demonized me, and, most often, it disqualified me. As early as my first year at the university, I measured the brutality of the course I proposed to follow and the titanic efforts I'd have to make in order to deserve my status as a full citizen. The diploma didn't resolve everything; I had to be charming and reassuring, I had to take blows without returning them, and I had to hold my tongue until my jaws ached because I couldn't afford to lose face. Thoroughly against my will, I found myself representing my community. To some extent, the community was the chief reason why I had to succeed. It hadn't been necessary for *my* people to send me on this mission; I was automatically designated for the thankless, perfidious job by the way *the others* looked at me.

I come from a poor but honest background, where salvation lay in keeping your word and living an upright life. My grandfather was the patriarch of our tribe. He possessed land but no ambition, and he didn't know that longevity depends not so much on the firmness of your undertakings as on the permanent reexamination of your own certitudes. He died despoiled, his eyes wide open, his heart broken with amazement and outrage. My father had no wish to inherit his father's blinkers. He had little enthusiasm for the peasant's condition; he wanted to be an artist—which, in his ancestral glossary, was defined as "dropout" and "loiterer." I can remember the monumental rows that took place whenever Grandfather caught my father painting a canvas in the shack he used as a makeshift studio while the other members of the family, young and old, were working themselves to exhaustion in the orchards. My father, with his Olympian calm, would declare that life was not only hoeing, pruning, watering, and picking; that it was painting, singing, and writing, as well; and teaching; and that the greatest of all vocations was *healing*. His dearest wish was for me to become a doctor. I've seldom seen anyone work so hard for his kid as he did for me. I was his only son. If he didn't want any others, it was so he could give me a maximum number of opportunities. He gave everything he had so he could offer the tribe its first physician. When he saw me brandishing my diploma, he threw himself into my arms like a stream into the sea. That day was the one and only time I ever saw tears on his cheeks. When he died, he was lying on a hospital bed, stroking my stethoscope—which I'd brought with me because I knew it gave him pleasure—as though it were a holy relic.

My father was a good person. He took things as they came and adjusted to them without artifice and without fanfare. He wasn't interested in taking the bull by the horns, and he didn't go into crisis mode when things got tight. As far as he was concerned, spells of bad luck weren't trials, just hitches. You had to go on past them, even if it meant a few minutes of suffering on the way through. His humility and his discernment were a gift. I wanted so much to be like him, to possess his frugality and his moderation! Thanks to him, even though I was growing up in a land that had been tormented since the dawn of time, I refused to consider the world as a battlefield. I could see that wars beget wars, that reprisals follow reprisals, but I forbade myself to give them any support of any kind. I didn't believe in prophecies of discord, and I couldn't bring myself to accept the notion that God could incite his subjects to take up arms against one another and reduce the exercise of faith to an absurd and frightening question of power relationships. And ever since then, I've trusted anyone who required a little of my blood to purify my soul about as much as I would trust a scorpion. I have no desire to believe in vales of tears or valleys of shadows—there are other more charming and less irrational features of the landscape all around me. My father said, "Anyone who tells you that a greater symphony exists than the breath in your body is lying. He wants to un-

dermine your most beautiful possession: the chance to
profit from every moment of your life. If you start from the
principle that your worst enemy is the very person who tries
to sow hatred in your heart, you're halfway to happiness.
All you have to do is reach out your hand and take the rest.
And remember this: There's nothing, *absolutely nothing*,
more important than your life. And your life isn't more important than other people's lives."

I've never forgotten that.

I've even made it my motto. I'm convinced that when
men finally subscribe to that way of thinking, they will at
last have reached maturity.

My little skirmishes with Navid helped put me back on
my feet. Although they haven't restored me to complete
clearheadedness, they've at least allowed me to look inside
myself with some detachment. My anger's still there, but
it's no longer stirring in my guts like a foreign body waiting
to be retched up and spewed out. Occasionally, when I sit
on the balcony, contemplating the traffic, I even find something appealing about it. Kim's not watching what she says
with the same excessive caution as she used three days ago.
She invents silly comic routines to get me to smile, and after she leaves for the hospital in the morning, I no longer
content myself with staying shut up in my room until she
returns. I've taken to going out and strolling about the
streets. I sit in cafés and smoke cigarettes, or I go to a
square and pick out a bench and watch the little kids frol-
icking in the sun. I don't yet have the nerve to get near a
newspaper; however, if I hear a radio broadcasting news

while I'm out strolling, I no longer dash to the other side of the street.

Ezra Benhaim came to visit me at Kim's place. Neither my hypothetical return to work nor Ilan Ros's name was mentioned. Ezra wanted to know how I was doing, how far along I was in getting over what happened. He took me to a restaurant to prove to me that it didn't bother him to be seen in my company. A dramatic gesture, but sincere. I insisted on paying for us both. After dinner—Kim was on duty—we went into a bar and got sloshed like two gods letting off steam after having used up all their anathemas.

————

"I have to go to Bethlehem."

The sound of clinking dishes in the kitchen comes to an abrupt stop. Kim waits a few seconds before showing her face in the doorway. She's got one eyebrow higher than the other as she stares at me.

I crush out my cigarette in the ashtray and get ready to light another one.

Kim dries her hands on a dishcloth hanging on the wall and joins me in the living room. She says, "Are you joking?"

"Do I look like I'm joking, Kim?"

She gives a little start. "Of course you're joking. What are you going to do in Bethlehem?"

"Sihem's letter was postmarked from there."

"So?"

"So I want to know what she was up to in Bethlehem

while I thought she was at her grandmother's house in Kafr Kanna."

Kim drops into the wicker chair opposite me. She's had enough of my unpredictable excursions. She takes deep breaths, as though forcing down her pique, chews her teeth in search of her words, finds none, and puts two fingers on each of her temples. "You're not being realistic, Amin. I don't know what's going through your head, but this is too much. There's no goddamned reason for you to go to Bethlehem."

"I've got a foster sister there. I'm positive Sihem went to her house before she carried out her insane mission. The letter's postmarked Friday the twenty-seventh, the day before the . . . the tragedy. I want to know who indoctrinated my wife, who strapped explosives on her and sent her to her target. There's no way I'm going to fold my arms or turn the page on something I can't get my mind around."

Kim's on the point of tearing out her hair. "Do you hear what you're saying? Let me remind you, we're talking about terrorists here. These are not people who bother with the niceties. You're a surgeon, not a cop. You have to leave this job to the police. They've got the appropriate tools and the personnel qualified to carry out this sort of investigation. If you want to know what happened to your wife, go find Navid and tell him about the letter."

"This is a personal matter. . . ."

"Bullshit! Seventeen people were killed and dozens of others wounded. There's nothing personal about this matter. It was a suicide attack, and suicide attacks come under the exclusive jurisdiction of the government. Leave the investigating to the proper authorities. In my opinion, you're about to go off the rails, Amin. If you really want to do something useful, give the letter to Navid. It may be the very clue the police are waiting for to break the case."

"That's out of the question. I don't like other people meddling in my business. I want to go to Bethlehem, alone. I don't need anyone else. I know people down there. I'll talk to them and prod them until they let something slip. I'll be able to force some of them to spill the beans."

"And afterward?"

"After what?"

"Let's say you succeed in forcing some of them to spill the beans. What's the next number on the program? Pulling their ears? Demanding payment, say damages and interest? Come on, you can't be serious. Sihem surely had a whole network behind her. She had logistical support; she went through some kind of training. You don't blow yourself up in a public place on a whim. That's the final step in a long period of brainwashing, of meticulous psychological and material preparation. Enormous precautions are taken before someone is sent into action. The commanders need to protect their bases and cover their tracks. They don't select their suicide bomber until they're absolutely sure of his determination and reliability. Now, I want you to picture yourself invading their territory and sniffing around their hideouts. You think they're going to wait politely until you make your way to where they are? They'll do away with you so fast, you won't even have time to realize what a boneheaded idea it was to play detective. I swear, I'm scared stiff at the mere prospect of imagining you crawling around that nest of vipers."

She grabs my hands, reviving the pain in my wrist.

"It's not a good idea, Amin."

"Maybe not, but I haven't been able to think of anything else since I read the letter."

"I understand, but this sort of thing isn't for you."

"Don't wear yourself out, Kim. You know how hard-headed I am."

She raises her arms to calm things down. "All right. Let's postpone the debate until this evening. I hope you'll have regained the power of sober thought by then."

When evening comes, she invites me to dinner in a restaurant on the beach. We sit on a terrace with the sea breeze lashing our faces. The sea is thick; there's something sententious in its sound. Kim perceives that she won't be able to make me change my mind. She picks at her food like a weary bird.

This is a pleasant place. It's run by a French immigrant, who offers informal meals in an agreeable setting, with picture windows as big as horizons, plush chairs upholstered in wine-red leather, and tables with embroidered place mats. A candle of imposing size burns away in a crystalline cup. There aren't many people here, but the other couples all seem to be regular customers. Their gestures are refined and their conversations discreet. Our host is a small, frail, lively fellow, immaculately dressed and exquisitely courteous. We've accepted his recommendations for the first course and the wine. Kim surely had something in mind when she invited me to this restaurant, but whatever that something was, she seems to have lost sight of it.

"It looks like you get a kick out of manipulating my blood-sugar level." She sighs, dropping her napkin as though throwing in the sponge.

"Put yourself in my place, Kim. This isn't just about what Sihem did. I'm in this, too. If my wife killed herself, that proves I wasn't able to make her prefer to live. I must certainly bear some part of the responsibility."

Kim tries to protest; I raise a hand by way of asking her not to interrupt me.

"It's true, Kim. There's no smoke without fire. I agree, she committed a crime, but laying the whole blame for it on her won't salve my conscience."

"You had nothing to do with it."

"Yes, I did. I was her husband. My duty was to watch over her and protect her. I'm sure she tried to attract my attention to the great wave that was threatening to sweep her away. I'd bet anything she tried to give me a sign. And while she was trying to get out of the trap she was in . . . Damn it! What was I thinking?"

"Did she really try to get out of it?"

"Why wouldn't she? You can't go to your destruction the way you go to a ball. Inevitably, just when you're preparing to take the fatal step, a seed of doubt sprouts in you. And it was that precise instant that I was incapable of detecting. Sihem surely wanted me to wake her up, to bring her back to herself, but my mind was elsewhere. And I'll never forgive myself for that."

I hasten to light a cigarette.

After a long silence, I say, "I don't get any amusement out of worrying you, Kim. I've lost my taste for joking. Ever since I read that damned letter, all I can think about is the sign I wasn't able to decipher at the time, the sign that remains a mystery today. There must have been a moment, there must have been a sign, and I want to remember it, don't you understand? I have to remember it. I have no other choice. Since I got that letter, I've been constantly rooting around in my memories, trying to find the right one. Whether I'm asleep or I'm awake, that's all I think about. I've passed everything in review, from the most unforgettable moments to the least fathomable words and the vaguest gestures; nothing. And this blank spot is driving me crazy. You can't imagine how much it tortures me, Kim. I can't go on like this, pursuing it and suffering it at the same time."

Kim doesn't know what to do with her little hands. She says, "Maybe Sihem didn't feel any need to give you a sign."

"That's impossible. She loved me. She couldn't ignore me to the point of not communicating anything to me."

"It wasn't up to her. She wasn't the same woman anymore, Amin. She wasn't allowed to make a mistake. Letting you in on her secret would have offended the gods and compromised her commitment. It's exactly like being in a religious sect. Nothing can filter out. The safety of the brotherhood rests on that imperative."

"Yes, but it was a question of death, Kim. Sihem had to die. She was aware of what that would signify both for her and for me. She was too dignified to pull the wool over my eyes like some kind of hypocrite. She gave me a sign; there's no doubt about it."

"Would that have changed anything?"

"Who knows?"

I take several drags on my cigarette, as though trying to stop it from going out. A knot forms in my throat, and a few words escape me: "I'm so unhappy, I can't believe it."

Kim sways, but she holds on.

I stub out the end of the cigarette in the ashtray.

"My father used to tell me, 'Keep your sorrows to yourself. They're all you have when you've lost everything else.' "

"Amin, please."

I ignore her and go on: "When a man's still in shock—and what a shock!—he's not likely to know exactly when his period of mourning ends and his life as a widower begins, but there are some boundaries he has to get past if he wants to go forward. Where are they? I don't know, but what I *do* know is that I have to move on. I can't just stay here feeling sorry for myself."

In my turn, and to my great amazement, I seize her hands and cover them with mine. It feels as though I have two crippled sparrows in the hollows of my palms. My grip is so cautious that Kim's shoulders tense up; her eyes shine with self-conscious tears, which she tries to hide behind a smile the likes of which I have never seen before.

"I'll be very careful," I promise her. "I have no intention of taking revenge or dismantling the network. I just want to understand why the love of my life excluded me from hers, why the woman I was crazy about was more receptive to other men's sermons than she was to my poems."

A tear spills out of my guardian angel's eye and suddenly rolls down over her cheekbone. Surprised and embarrassed, Kim moves to wipe it away, but I'm quicker than she is, and my finger gathers the tear the moment it reaches the corner of her mouth.

"You're a wonderful person, Kim."

"I know," she says, and then, halfway through a sob, she bursts out laughing.

I take her hands again and squeeze them very hard. "I don't have to tell you that I wouldn't have made it through this without you."

"Not tonight, Amin. . . . Maybe another time."

Her lips tremble in their sad smile. Her eyes lock onto mine in an effort to get rid of the emotion that's clouding them. I return her gaze intensely, without noticing that I'm twisting her fingers.

"Thanks," I say.

9.

———————————

As a trade-off for allowing me to take such flagrant risks, Kim insisted on driving me to Bethlehem. She said she wanted to be at my side. If only to serve as my chauffeur, she added. My wrist isn't completely recovered yet, and it's still hard for me to lift a bag or hold on to a steering wheel.

I tried to dissuade her, but she refused to budge.

Her brother Benjamin owns a second home in Jerusalem, and Kim proposed that we set up there, at least at first; once we're in place, she said, we can decide on the next steps as the situation develops. I wanted to leave right away. She requested enough time to operate on a patient and ask Ezra Benhaim for a week's leave of absence. When Ezra tried to penetrate the reasons behind her sudden departure, Kim told him she needed some rest and rehabilitation. Ezra didn't insist further.

So the day after the operation, we stuff our two travel bags into the trunk of her Nissan, pass by my house to pick up some personal effects and a few recent photographs of Sihem, and set out for Jerusalem.

We stop only once, to get some food and drink in a greasy spoon on the highway. The weather's fine, and the traffic's so heavy, it makes us think of the summer holiday rush.

We pass through Jerusalem as in a waking dream. It's the first time I've seen the city in about a dozen years. Its frenetic animation and its bustling, crowded shops recall memories I thought I'd left on the scrap heap. Images flash though my mind, sharp and gleaming, and mingle with the scents of the old town. It was in this age-old city that I saw my mother for the last time. She'd come to pray at her dying brother's bedside. His funeral brought together the entire tribe; some people came from countries so far away that their names threw the old folks into confusion. My mother didn't long survive the loss of the person she considered her real reason for living—my father had been a negligent husband, and I, her son, had been stolen from her by my years away at school and my extensive travels.

Benjamin's place—on the outskirts of town, among other squat buildings with sunburned walls—seems to turn its back on the legendary city and focus on the orchards that run up and down the rocky hills. The house is discreetly situated, withdrawn from the world and its disorders; somewhere in the distance you can hear the sound of squealing kids at play, but they're not visible anywhere. Benjamin is in Tel Aviv, so Kim follows his instructions and finds the keys under the third flowerpot from the entrance to the patio. The house is small and low, with a loggia overlooking a shadowy little courtyard jealously protected by a greedy climbing vine. A sculpted fountain with a bronze lion's head overhangs a bramble-choked rivulet, which runs past a wrought-iron bench clumsily painted green. Kim assigns me to a bedroom next to a study filled with books and manuscripts. There's a folding bed with a mattress that leaves something to be desired, a Formica table, and a stool. A worn-out, threadbare carpet does its best to camouflage the cracks in the floor, which was apparently laid in biblical times. I throw my bag on the bed and wait until Kim comes out of the bathroom so I can tell her what my plans are.

"Rest for a while first," she says.

"I'm not tired. It's noon, a good time to find somebody home at my foster sister's house. There's no need for you to disturb yourself—I'll take a taxi."

"I have to go with you."

"Kim, please. If I have problems, I'll call you on your cell phone and tell you where to come and pick me up. I don't think I'll run into any trouble today. I just want to visit family and friends and reconnoiter the ground."

Kim grumbles before she lets me go.

———

Bethlehem has changed a great deal since the last time I passed through here, more than ten years ago. Hordes of refugees, abandoning their homes in towns and villages lately transformed into shooting ranges, have swelled the

population, and Bethlehem now features new conglomera-
tions of cinder-block hovels built one against the other, like
barricades. Most of these miserable dwellings stand unfin-
ished, covered with sheet metal or bristling with scrap iron,
their facades pierced by haggard windows and grotesque
doors. You'd think you were at a huge collection point,
where all the wretched of the earth have arranged to meet
in a futile quest for absolution.

Leaning on canes, with kaffiyehs on their heads and
faded vests under their open jackets, emaciated old men are
daydreaming in front of their houses, some sitting on stools,
others on steps. They gaze into the distance and seem to listen to nothing but their memories, impregnable in their silence and undisturbed by the mighty racket of the urchins
around them, squabbling at the top of their voices.

I have to ask the way several times before a little boy
leads me to a big house with crumbling walls. He waits
politely until I drop a few coins into his hand, and then
vanishes. I knock on an old worm-eaten wooden door and
prick up my ears. I hear the sound of slippers shuffling
across the floor; then a latch clicks and the door is opened
by a woman with a pale, troubled face. It takes me forever
to recognize her: it's Leila, my foster sister. She's a little over
forty-five, but she looks sixty. Her hair has turned white and
her features have gone slack; you'd think she was dying.

She scrutinizes me in confusion.

"It's Amin," I say.

She starts, then says, "My God!" as though suddenly
coming to her senses.

We fling ourselves against each other. As I hold her tightly against me, I can feel her sobs rising up one by one from her chest and spreading over her frail body in a multitude of vibrations. She takes a step back to contemplate me, her face wet with tears. As a sign of gratitude, she recites a verse from the Qur'an, and then she throws herself into my arms again.

"Come," she says. "You're just in time to share a meal with me."

"Thanks, but I'm not hungry. Are you here alone?"

"Yes. Yasser doesn't come home until evening."

"And your children?"

"Well, they've grown up since you saw them, you know? The girls are married, and Adel and Mahmoud are off on their own."

There's a silence, and then Leila bows her head. "It must be so hard for you," she says in a toneless voice.

"It's the worst thing that could happen to a man," I admit.

"I can imagine. I've thought about you a lot since the attack. I know how sensitive and fragile you are, and I wondered how someone so thin-skinned could get over such a . . . such a . . ."

"Disaster," I say, coming to her aid. "Because that's what it is, a disaster, and not a small one, either. I've come here expressly to find out more about it. I didn't know anything about Sihem's plans—frankly, I didn't have the slightest suspicion of them. And her death seems like such a tragedy. . . . It's literally crushed me."

"Don't you want to sit down?"

"No. Tell me, how was she before she set out to do what she did?"

"What do you mean?"

"How did she act? Did she seem to be aware of what she was going to do? Do you think she looked normal, or was there something strange about her?"

"I didn't see her."

"She was in Bethlehem on Friday the twenty-seventh, the day before the attack."

"I know, but she didn't stay long. I was with my eldest daughter—it was her son's circumcision. I learned about the attack in the car on the way home."

Suddenly, she claps her hand to her lips as though to prevent herself from saying anything more. "Good God!" she says. "What a blabbermouth!" She looks at me with terrified eyes. "Why have you come to Bethlehem?"

"I've already told you."

She totters, clasping her forehead between her thumb and her index finger. I seize her by the waist to stop her from collapsing and help her sit down on the padded bench behind her.

"Amin, my brother, I don't think I have the right to talk about these things. I swear to you, I don't really know what's going on. If Yasser finds out I haven't held my tongue, he'll cut it off. I was surprised to see you, and I let some words slip out that didn't belong to me. Do you understand what I'm saying, Amin?"

"I'll act as though you haven't said anything. But I have

to know what my wife was up to in your neighborhood and who she was working with."

"Have the police sent you?"

"Let me remind you that Sihem was my wife."

Leila's thinking clearly now, and she's bitterly angry with herself. "I wasn't here, Amin. That's the real truth. You can verify it yourself. I went to my eldest daughter's house for her son's circumcision. Your aunts and your cousins were there, and so were lots of other family members and friends you must know. That Friday, I wasn't home."

I see that she's about to panic and hasten to reassure her: "Calm down, Leila. It's only me, your brother. I'm not carrying any weapons or handcuffs. I'd hate to cause you any problems, as you well know. And I'm not here to bring down trouble on your family, either. Where can I find Yasser? I want him to be the one who answers my questions."

Leila implores me not to tell her husband about our conversation. I promise I won't. She gives me the address of the pressing shed where Yasser works and walks me to the street to see me off.

I look for a taxi around the square but don't see any. At the end of half an hour, just as I'm preparing to give Kim a call, an unauthorized driver offers to drop me off wherever I want for a few shekels. He's a fairly stocky young man, with laughing eyes and a fanciful little goatee. He opens the door for me with theatrical obsequiousness and practically pushes me into one of the leprous seats in his rattletrap "taxi."

We drive around the square, turn into a road scored by

deep fissures, and exit the town. After a slalom in the midst of some headlong traffic, we strike out cross-country until we reach a dirt road up in the hills.

"You're not from around here?" the driver asks me.

"No."

"Visiting relatives, or on business?"

"Both."

"You come from far away?"

"I don't know."

The driver nods his head. "You're not the talkative type," he says.

"Not today."

"I see."

We go a few miles on the dusty road without encountering a living soul. The sun beats down hard on the stony hillocks, which seem to be hiding behind one another in order to spy on us.

The driver speaks again. "Me, I can't function with tape on my mouth. If I don't talk, I explode."

I keep quiet.

He clears his throat and goes on: "I've never seen anyone with hands so immaculate and well manicured as yours. Are you a doctor, by any chance? Only doctors take such good care of their hands."

I turn toward the orchards, which spread out as far as the eye can see.

Annoyed by my silence, the driver breathes a sigh. Then he rummages around in the glove compartment, extracts a cassette tape, and immediately slips it into the player.

"Listen to this, my friend," he says excitedly. "If you've never heard Sheikh Marwan preach, you're missing half your life."

He turns a knob to increase the volume. The car is filled with a hubbub of voices, punctuated by ecstatic cries and wild applause. Someone—probably the speaker—taps on the microphone to quiet the crowd. The uproar gradually subsides, flaring up here and there until an attentive silence greets the limpid voice of Imam Marwan.

"Is there a splendor so great as the Lord's face, my brothers? Down here in this changeable, flimsy world, are there other splendors great enough to turn us away from the face of Allah? Tell me which splendors they might be. The tawdry illusions that attract the simpleminded and the wretched? The snares and lures? The mirages that hide the trapdoor to the place of the damned, the mirages that blind the deluded and doom them forever? Tell me which splendors, my brothers. And on the last day, when dust is all that shall remain of the earth, when all that shall remain of our illusions is the ruin of our souls, what answer shall we have to the question, What have we done with our existence? What answer shall we have when we are asked, all of us, great and small, What have you done with your life? What have you done with my holy prophets and my generous gifts? What have you done with the salvation I entrusted to you? And on that day, my brothers, your fortunes, your relations, your allies, your supporters will give you no help." (The crowd sets up a clamor, which is quickly dominated by the sheikh's voice.) "In truth, my brothers, a man's riches are not what he possesses, but what he leaves behind him. And what do we possess, my brothers? What are we going to leave behind us? A homeland? What homeland? A history? What history? Some monuments? Where are they? By your ancestors, show them to me! Every day, we are dragged through the mud or before the courts. Every day, tanks roll over our feet, overturn our carts, smash our houses, and fire without warning on our children. Every day, the whole world witnesses our misfortune. . . ."

My arm decompresses and my thumb mashes the eject button, popping out the cassette. The driver is thunderstruck. His eyes bulge, his mouth opens wide, and he cries out, "What are you doing?"

"I don't like sermons."

"What?" Indignation chokes him. "You don't believe in God?"

"I don't believe in his holy men."

He slams on the brakes so hard, his wheels lock up and the car skates sideways for a few meters before it comes to a stop, straddling the road. "Are you mad?" the driver growls, livid with rage. "How dare you raise your hand against Sheikh Marwan?"

"I have the right. . . ."

"You have no right! No right! You're in *my* automobile. And whether inside my car or out of it, I will not allow a disgusting piece of shit to put his filthy paws on Sheikh Marwan! Now get out of my car and out of my sight."

"We haven't arrived yet."

"Oh, yes, we have. End of the line! You get your sorry ass

out of my car or I'll tear the skin off of it with my bare hands!" Whereupon he utters a curse, leans across me, furiously opens my door, and starts shoving me outside.

"And you'd better hope our paths don't cross again, you son of a bitch," he says threateningly. With a vicious yank, he slams the door closed, guns the car backward, makes a half turn toward Bethlehem, and roars away amid a dissonant flurry of backfires.

I stand agape in the middle of the road and watch as the car disappears from sight.

Then I sit down on a rock and wait for a vehicle to pass. When nothing comes, I get up and continue on foot until a carter catches up with me several miles farther on.

Yasser goes weak in the knees when he sees me standing on the threshold of the shed, where two teenagers are bustling around the press and keeping an eye on the thick streams of olive oil cascading into the collection vat.

"What a surprise!" he exclaims between two exaggerated bouts of hugging and kissing. "Our surgeon, in the flesh. Why didn't you tell us you were coming? I would have sent someone to welcome your arrival."

His enthusiasm is too embarrassed to be credible. He consults his watch, turns to the teenagers, and tells them loudly that he's going to have to absent himself for a while and that he's counting on them to finish the work. Then he takes me by the arm and guides me to an old van parked under a tree at the foot of the mound the press is on.

"Let's go to the house," he says. "Leila will be delighted to see you again. Or have you seen her already?"

"Yasser," I say, "let's not beat around the bush. I have neither the time nor the inclination. I've come here for a specific reason." I'm brusque with him, hoping to surprise him into saying something. "I know Sihem was in Bethlehem and at your house the day before the attack."

"Who told you that?" he asks in a panicked voice, all the while casting terrified looks in the direction of the pressing shed.

I take the letter out of my shirt pocket and lie: "Sihem told me, that very day."

A spasm begins in the area around his cheekbone. He swallows hard and then begins mumbling. "She didn't stay long. It was just a quick visit to say hello. Leila wasn't home—she was with our daughter in Ein Kerem—and your wife didn't even want to take a cup of tea. She left after no more than a quarter of an hour. She hadn't come to Bethlehem for us. That Friday, Sheikh Marwan was expected to speak in the Grand Mosque. Your wife wanted him to bless her. It was only when we saw her picture in the newspaper that we understood."

He takes me by the shoulders like a wrestler and speaks confidingly: "We're all very proud of her."

I know he's said that because he's trying to treat me gently, or maybe because he wants to cajole me. Yasser doesn't know how to keep his cool; the smallest unforeseen problem unsettles him.

"Proud that she threw herself away?"

He jumps as though he's been bitten. "Threw herself away?"

"Or blew herself away, if you prefer."

"I don't like these phrases."

"All right, I'll rephrase my question: What pride can you take in sending people to die so others can live free and happy?"

He raises his hands in front of his chest, imploring me to lower my voice because of his teenage helpers—we're still too close to them for his comfort. He signals me to follow him around to the other side of the van and walks ahead nervously, stumbling a little with every step.

I keep harassing him: "And besides, why?"

"Why what?"

His fear, his destitution, his filthy clothes, his badly shaven face, and his rheumy eyes fill me with a brutal, growing anger. My body vibrates from head to foot. "Why," I grumble, upset by my own words, "why sacrifice some for the benefit of others? It's generally the best and the bravest who choose to lay down their lives for the sake of those who hide in their holes. So why favor the sacrifice of the righteous in order to permit the less righteous to survive them? Don't you think that's a way of weakening the human species? What's going to be left of it in a few generations if it's always the best who are called upon to exit the scene so that the cowards, the counterfeits, the charlatans, and the pricks can continue to proliferate like rats?"

"Amin, you're not making sense to me. Things have always been this way since the beginning of time. Some die so others can be saved. You don't believe in the salvation of others?"

"Not when it damns mine. Look, you and your friends have fucked up my life, destroyed my home, ruined my career, and turned everything I built—by the sweat of my brow, stone for stone—into dust. From one day to the next, my dreams collapsed like a house of cards. Poof! Gone with the wind! I've lost *everything* for *nothing*. Did any of you think about my suffering when you were jumping for joy at the news that the creature I treasured most in the world was dead, that she'd detonated a bomb in a restaurant filled with kids? And you, you want to make me believe I should consider myself the happiest of men because my wife is a heroine, because she gave up her life, her comfort, and my love without even consulting me or preparing me for the worst? What did I look like while I was refusing to admit what everyone knew? A cuckold! I looked like a pitiful cuckold, that's what I looked like. Like an object of ridicule. Like a man who works and slaves to make life as pleasant as possible for the woman he loves, while she's cheating on him the whole time."

"I think you're talking to the wrong person. I don't have anything to do with any of this. I didn't know what Sihem's plans were. It would never have occurred to me that she was capable of taking such a step."

"Didn't you tell me you were proud of her?"

"What else could I say? I didn't know you didn't know what she planned to do."

"You think I would have encouraged her to make this kind of spectacle of herself if I'd had the least notion of her intentions?"

"I'm really confused, Amin. Forgive me if I've—if I've—ah, I don't understand anything anymore. I—I don't know what to say."

"In that case, don't talk. If you keep quiet, at least you don't run the risk of saying something idiotic."

10.

———————

Yasser. It pains me to look at him, distraught as he is, hunkering down inside his raggedy shirt collar as if he's expecting the sky to fall on his head. He pretends to concentrate on the road so he won't have to meet my eyes. Obviously, I'm barking up the wrong tree. Yasser's not the kind of guy you can count on when things get hard, and it's even less likely that he'd be associated with preparations for a slaughter. He's past sixty now, just a wreck with red-rimmed eyes and a sagging mouth, liable to drop dead on me if I frown at him too hard. If he says he knows nothing about the attack, it must be true. Yasser never takes any risks. I don't remember ever having seen him grumble, much less roll up his sleeves for a fight. On the contrary, he's far more inclined to withdraw into his shell and wait until things settle down than to utter anything resembling a protest. His irrational fear of cops and his blind submission to the authority of the state have reduced him to survival on its most basic level: He works like a horse and considers every mouthful of bread a gesture of defiance in the face of bad luck. And now, when I see him crouched over his steering wheel, with his wizened neck and his low profile, already feeling guilty, if only because he was in my path, I realize fully the senselessness of my enterprise. But how do I put out these red-hot embers I've got burning holes in my guts? How can I look at myself in a mirror and not cover my face, with my self-esteem in shreds and this doubt that's still here, subverting my grief, despite what I know to be true? Ever since Captain Moshé released me to my own devices, I can't close my eyes without finding myself face-to-face with Sihem's smile. She was so loving and so considerate, and when we'd stand together in our garden, my arm around her waist, and I'd tell her about the wonderful days that lay ahead of us and the grand projects I was working on for her, she seemed to hang on my words. I can still feel her fingers squeezing mine with what I thought was indestructible passion and conviction. She was a firm believer in our bright future, and every time I lost heart, she redoubled her efforts. We were so happy; we had such confidence in each other. What spell has made the monument I was building around her vanish, like a sand castle under the waves? How can I continue to have faith, after putting all my confidence into a sacred vow that turns out to be as unreliable as a quack physician's promise? It's because I have no answer to these questions that I've come to Bethlehem to tempt fate, inconsolable as I am, and naked, and suicidal in my turn.

Yasser explains that he has to leave his van in a garage because the little alley that leads to his house is inaccessible to cars. He's relieved that he's finally found something to say that entails no risk of blundering. I tell him to park his heap wherever the hell he feels like. He nods as though delivered from an unbearable burden and turns into a street teeming with people. We go through a chaotic neighborhood before reaching a broad, dusty esplanade, where a kabob vendor is busy keeping the flies away from his meat. The garage in question stands at the corner of a narrow little street, across from a lot littered with broken crates and shards of glass. After Yasser blows the horn twice, we have to wait several minutes before we hear the sound of bolts being drawn. A large sliding door painted a distressing shade of blue moves aside with a metallic shriek. Yasser backs and fills, aiming the nose of his van at a sort of covered yard, and slips adroitly between the carcass of a miniature crane and a mutilated 4×4. The hoary-headed, slovenly watchman greets us with an enervated wave of his hand, closes the door again, and goes on about his business.

"This used to be an abandoned warehouse," Yasser informs me, glad of a new subject. "My son Adel bought it for a song. His plan was to turn it into a mechanic's shop. But our people are so resourceful and so indifferent to maintaining the jalopies they ride around in that the shop went broke pretty soon. Adel lost a lot of money in that business. While he's waiting on some other opportunities, he's transformed the warehouse into a parking lot for local residents."

A dozen automobiles are waiting quietly here and there.

Some are out of commission, with burst tires and bashed-in windshields. My attention is drawn by a large, powerful car parked a little off to one side, in a spot shaded from the sun. It's an old cream-colored Mercedes, half-covered by a tarpaulin.

"That belongs to Adel," Yasser informs me proudly, following my gaze.

"When did he buy it?"

"I don't remember."

"Why is it up on blocks? Is it a collector's item?"

"No, but when Adel isn't here, no one takes it out."

Voices overlay one another in my head. Captain Moshé's comes first—*He didn't get the car's license number, but he says it was an older-model Mercedes, cream-colored*—drowned out by Navid Ronnen's—*My father-in-law has one like that.*

"So where's Adel?"

"You know how these wheeler-dealers are, one day here, the next day somewhere else, always tracking down the big score."

My relatives rarely visited us in Tel Aviv, but Adel was an exception; he stopped by frequently. Young and dynamic, he was always determined to succeed, at whatever price. He wasn't yet seventeen when he proposed that I invest in some telephone-related deal with him. Seeing my reluctance, he didn't press the issue, but not long afterward he returned to present me with a second project. This time, the business he wanted to go into was the recycling of spare parts for automobiles. I was at great pains to explain to him that I was a surgeon and that I had no other vocation. In those days, he would come to my house every time he passed through Tel Aviv. He was a fantastic, amusing fellow, and Sihem adopted him without a struggle. He dreamed about starting some sort of enterprise in Beirut, from where he would spread out to conquer the entire Arab market, particularly including the monarchies of the Persian Gulf. Lately, however—for more than a year, in fact—I haven't seen him.

"When Sihem came to your house, was Adel with her?"

Yasser nervously strokes the bridge of his nose.

"I don't know. When she showed up, I was at the mosque for Friday prayers. The only person who saw her was my grandson Issam, who was house-sitting."

"You said she didn't even stay for a cup of tea."

"Just a manner of speaking."

"And Adel?"

"I don't know."

"Does Issam know?"

"I didn't ask him."

"Did Issam know my wife?"

"I suppose so."

"And since when? Sihem had never set foot in Bethlehem before, and none of you has ever come to our house."

Yasser becomes confused; his hands get lost in vague gestures. "Let's go to the house, Amin. We'll have a nice cup of tea and talk about all this calmly."

At the house, things become more complicated. We find Leila in bed, with a neighbor standing by. Leila's pulse is weak. I suggest that we take her to the nearest clinic at once. Yasser refuses, explaining to me that my foster sister is following a course of treatment; it's the pills she takes in large quantities daily, he says, that have reduced her to this state. A little later, after Leila falls asleep, I tell Yasser that I insist on having a chat with Issam.

"All right," Yasser says without enthusiasm. "I'll go find him. He lives two blocks from here."

Twenty minutes later, Yasser's back, accompanied by a young boy with a sallow complexion. "He's sick," Yasser informs me.

"In that case, you shouldn't have brought him."

This is too much for Yasser. He mutters, "I thought we'd gone too far for that. . . ."

I don't learn a lot from Issam. Apparently, his grandfather rehearsed him before presenting him to me. According to Issam, Sihem arrived alone. She wanted to write something, and she asked for paper and a pen. Issam tore out a page from his school notebook and loaned her his ballpoint. When Sihem finished writing, she handed him a letter and asked him to post it for her. Issam left the house on this errand at once. As he stepped outside, he noticed a man on the street corner. He doesn't remember what the man looked like, but he's sure it wasn't anyone from the neighborhood. When Issam came back from the post office, Sihem had left and the stranger was gone.

"You were alone in the house?"

"Yes. Grandmother was in Ein Kerem, at my aunt's house. Grandfather was at the mosque. I did my homework while I was watching the house."

"Did you know Sihem?"

"I saw some pictures of her in Adel's photo album."

"And you recognized her right away?"

"Not right away. But the pictures came back to me when she told me who she was. She didn't want to see anyone in particular. She just wanted to sit down and write a letter before she left."

"How did she look?"

"Beautiful."

"That's not what I mean. Did she seem to be in a hurry or anything like that?"

Issam thinks for a moment.

"She looked normal."

"And that's all?"

Issam consults his grandfather with his eyes and has nothing more to say.

I turn abruptly on Yasser and assail him. "You say you didn't see her. Issam doesn't tell us anything we don't already know. So how can you tell me my wife was in Bethlehem to receive Sheikh Marwan's blessing?"

"Any child in the town can tell you the same thing," he replies. "The whole of Bethlehem knows Sihem came through here the day before the attack. She's become something of a local icon. Some people are even swearing they spoke to her and kissed her forehead. Reactions of that sort are common among us. A martyr is an open door to all sorts of tale telling. So the rumor may be an exaggeration, but according to what everyone says, Sihem was blessed by Sheikh Marwan that Friday."

"They met at the Grand Mosque?"

"Not during the prayer. Much later, after all the worshipers had gone home."

"I see."

————

Quite early the next day, I present myself at the Grand Mosque. Some men are at the end of their prayers, prostrating themselves on the broad quilts that cover the floor; a few others are reading the Qur'an, each in his own corner. I take off my shoes outside the sanctuary and cross the threshold. When I ask an old man if there's anyone in charge here I could talk to, he shrinks away from me, outraged that anyone would disturb him while he was at prayer. I look around to see if I can spot someone who looks likely to help me.

"Yes?" snaps a voice behind my back.

The voice belongs to a very tall young man with an emaciated face, deep-set eyes, and a hooked nose. I extend a hand, which he does not take. My face tells him nothing useful, so he's mystified by my intrusion.

"Dr. Amin Jaafari."

"Yes?"

"I'm Dr. Amin Jaafari."

"I heard you. What can I do for you?"

"My name means nothing to you?"

He gives me an evasive look. "I don't believe so."

"I'm Sihem Jaafari's husband."

The religious young man squints a little, pondering my words. Then, all at once, his forehead creases and his complexion turns a shade grayer. He puts his hand over his heart and exclaims, "My God! What was I thinking?"

There follows an effusive sequence of apologies. "My conduct was unpardonable."

"Forget about it."

He spreads out his arms and embraces me. "Brother Amin, it's an honor and a privilege to meet you. I shall go at once and announce you to the imam. I'm sure he'll be delighted to receive you."

He requests that I wait in the sanctuary, goes behind the *minbar*, lifts a curtain leading to a concealed inner room, and disappears. The few men who were reading with their backs to the wall consider me with curiosity. They didn't hear my name, but they noticed how the pious young man's attitude changed abruptly, and they saw him hurry off to alert his master. A large bearded fellow decisively lays his Qur'an aside and stares at me so imperturbably, he makes me uncomfortable.

I think I see part of the curtain being lifted and held aside, but no one appears from behind the *minbar*. Five minutes later, the imam's young assistant returns, his feelings visibly hurt. "I'm extremely sorry," he says. "The imam is not in. He must have gone out without my noticing."

He realizes that the other believers are watching us and gives them a black look that compels them to avert their eyes.

"Will he be back for the prayer?"

"Of course," he replies. Then, quickly recovering, he adds, "I don't know where he's gone. It may be that he won't return for several hours."

"That's all right. I'll just wait for him here."

The pious young man casts an uneasy glance in the direction of the *minbar*, swallows hard, and says, "There's no guarantee he'll be back before nightfall."

"That's not a problem. I'm willing to wait."

Overmatched, he shrugs, lifting his arms, and withdraws.

I sit down cross-legged at the foot of a column, pick up a book of hadiths, lay it in my lap, and open it at random. The imam's young assistant reappears, pretends to engage an old man in conversation, and then paces around the great prayer hall like a beast in a cage. Eventually, he steps out into the street.

One hour passes, and then a second. Around noon, three young men appear out of nowhere, come up to me, and perform the customary unctuous courtesies. Then they inform me that my presence in the mosque can serve no purpose and request that I leave the premises.

"I want to see the imam."

"The imam is unwell. He fell sick this morning. He won't be back for several days."

"I'm Dr. Amin Jaafari. . . ."

"That's fine," says the smallest of the three, interrupting me. He's a young fellow around thirty years old, with prominent cheekbones and a long scar across his forehead. "Now go back home."

"Not before I talk to the imam."

"We'll let you know as soon as he's feeling better."

"You know where to reach me?"

"Everyone in Bethlehem knows that."

They guide me politely but firmly to the exit, wait for me to put on my shoes, and escort me in silence to the corner of the street.

————

Two of the three men who saw me out of the mosque continue to follow me—ostentatiously—while I walk toward the center of town. They want me to know they have their eye on me and it's in my best interest to keep on walking.

It's market day. The square is packed with people. I walk into a dark café, order black coffee, no sugar, take a seat by a small window smudged with fingerprints and bug shit, and watch the teeming souk. The café is furnished with rudimentary tables and creaking chairs; a group of old men sit about under the lifeless eye of the server, who's wedged in behind his counter. At the table next to mine, a neat-looking gentleman in his fifties draws on his narghile. Farther on, some youngsters are playing a noisy game of dominoes. I hunker down in there until the prayer hour. When I hear the muezzin's call, I decide to go back to the Grand Mosque, hoping to catch the imam in the middle of the service.

As I enter the part of town where the mosque is, I'm intercepted by the two men who followed me this morning. They're not happy to see me, and they won't let me get anywhere near the sacred precincts. "What you're doing is not good, Doctor," the taller of the two says.

I go back to Leila's and wait for the next prayer.

Once again, I'm stopped before I reach the mosque. This time, there's a third man with my guardian angels, who are distinctly irritated by my obstinacy. The new fellow is well dressed, small but sturdy-looking, with a thin mustache and a large silver-plated ring on his finger. He asks me to follow him into a blind alley, and there, protected from inquiring eyes, he asks me what I think I'm trying to do.

"I'm asking to speak with the imam."

"On what subject?"

"You know very well why I'm here."

"Perhaps I do, but you don't know what you're stepping into."

The threat is clear; his eyes try to gouge mine. "For the love of heaven, Doctor," he says, his nerves fraying. "Do what you were told to do: Go back home."

He leaves me standing there and goes away, closely followed by his companions. I return to Yasser's house and wait for the Maghreb prayer, resolved to drive the imam into a corner this time. While I'm waiting, Kim calls me up. I reassure her and promise to call her back before evening.

The sun disappears on tiptoe behind the horizon. The street noise dies down. A little breeze rushes into the patio, which has baked all afternoon in the sun. Yasser comes home a few minutes before the prayer. He's annoyed to find me in his house but relieved to learn that I'm not staying the night.

At the call of the muezzin, I leave the house and direct my steps toward the mosque for the third time. The temple guards are not waiting for me in their den; they pounce on me about a block away from Yasser's house. There are five of them. Two stand lookout at the end of the alleyway while the other three shove me into a carriage entrance.

"You shouldn't play with fire, Doctor," says one of them, a tall, strapping young man, as he pins me against a wall.

I struggle to get out of his grip; his Herculean muscles do not yield. In the gathering darkness, his eyes throw off terrifying sparks.

"This number of yours isn't impressing anyone, Doctor," he says.

"My wife met the imam, Sheikh Marwan, in the Grand Mosque. That's the reason why I want an audience with him."

"You've been told a pack of lies. You're not wanted here."

"In what way am I bothering you?"

My question amuses and annoys him at the same time. He leans over my shoulder and whispers in my ear, "You're about to bring down a shitstorm on the whole fucking town."

"Watch your language," the small one says, the one with the prominent cheekbones and the scar on his forehead who spoke to me earlier at the mosque. "We're not in a pigsty."

The lout swallows his zeal and steps back. Upbraided and put in his place, he stands off to one side and has no more to say.

The small man addresses me in a conciliatory tone: "Dr.

Amin Jaafari, I'm certain you don't realize how much difficulty your presence in Bethlehem is causing. People here have become far too touchy. They choose to remain on guard so they won't have to respond to provocations. The Israelis are looking for any excuse to break up our communities and force us into ghettos. We know this, and we're trying not to commit the error they're anticipating so eagerly. And *you* are playing right into their hands."

He looks me straight in the eye and says, "We have nothing to do with your wife."

"But—"

"Please, Dr. Jaafari. Try to understand my position."

"My wife met Sheikh Marwan here in Bethlehem."

"Yes, that is indeed what people say, but it's not true. Sheikh Marwan hasn't visited us here for ages. Rumors of his presence are spread to defend him from ambushes. Every time he wants to make an appearance somewhere, the word goes out that he's in Haifa, Bethlehem, Jenin, Gaza, Nuseirat, Ramallah, everywhere at the same time, in order to cover his tracks and protect his movements. The Israeli security services are hot on his heels. They've deployed a whole contingent of informers who'll sound the alarm as soon as he shows his face outdoors. Two years ago, he miraculously escaped when a radio-guided missile was fired at him from a helicopter. Our cause has lost many prominent figures that way. Remember how the Israelis targeted Sheikh Yassin, in the fullness of his age and confined to a wheelchair. We have to watch over the few leaders we have left, Dr. Jaafari. And your behavior is no help to us."

He puts a hand on my shoulder and goes on: "Your wife is a martyr. We will be eternally grateful to her. But that fact does not authorize you to disparage her sacrifice or to put anyone else in danger. We respect your grief; respect our struggle."

"I want to know—"

"It's still too soon, Dr. Jaafari," he says in a peremptory tone, cutting me off. "I beg you, go back to Tel Aviv."

He gives his men a sign to leave us.

Once we're alone, he and I, he takes me by the neck with both hands, stands on tiptoe, kisses me voraciously on the forehead, and goes away without looking back.

11.

When the doorbell sounds, Kim rushes to the door and opens it immediately, without asking who's there. "God in heaven!" she cries. "Where have you been?"

She makes sure I'm steady on my feet, checks my face and my clothes for signs of violence, and shows me the backs of her hands. "Bravo!" she says. "Thanks to you, I've gone back to biting my nails."

"I couldn't find a regular taxi in Bethlehem, and the Israelis are manning their checkpoints, so no illegal driver would offer me a ride, either."

"You could've called me. I would've gone to get you."

"You wouldn't have been able to find the way. Bethlehem's a big jumble of a town. There's a maze of streets and alleys. And a sort of curfew goes into force after dark. I didn't know where I could tell you to meet me."

"Well," she says, moving aside to let me pass, "at least you're in one piece."

We walk out onto the loggia, where she's put a table. As she begins to set it, she explains, "I bought some groceries while you were gone. Have you had dinner? I hope not, because I'm cooking up a little feast."

"I'm dying of hunger."

"Good news," she says.

"I perspired a lot today."

"I figured you might. The bathroom's ready for you."

I go to my room and get my toilet kit.

I stand under a scalding hot shower for about twenty minutes, with my hands against the wall, my back rounded, and my chin on my chest. The water streaming over my body soothes me. I feel my muscles relax, and my breathing calms down. Kim comes and hands me a bathrobe around the side of the shower curtain. Her exaggerated modesty makes me smile. I dry myself with an enormous towel, vigorously rubbing arms and legs, put on the robe—it's Benjamin's, too big for me—and join Kim on the loggia.

I've hardly sat down on a chair when someone rings the doorbell. Kim and I look at each other quizzically. "Are you expecting visitors?" I ask.

"Not that I know of," she says, getting up to open the door.

A big fellow wearing a yarmulke and an undershirt practically pushes Kim out of his way. He takes a quick look over her head, spots me, and says, "I'm your neighbor in apartment thirty-eight. I saw your light and thought I'd come tell Benjamin hello."

"Benjamin's not here," Kim says, irritated by the intruder's nonchalance. "I'm his sister, Dr. Kim Yehuda."

"His sister? I've never seen you."

"You're seeing me now."

He nods and turns his gaze back to me. "Well," he says, "I hope I haven't disturbed you."

"No problem."

He brings a finger to his forehead in a vague salute and withdraws. Before closing the door, Kim steps outside to watch him leave.

As she comes back to the table, she grumbles, "What nerve!"

We start eating. The insect noises of the night intensify on all sides. An enormous moth whirls madly around the light shining on the courtyard behind the apartment. In the sky, where so many love songs used to float in days of old, a crescent moon noses into a cloud. There's a low wall surrounding the back of the building, and beyond it we can see the lights of Jerusalem, with its minarets and its church towers now cleft asunder by that sacrilegious, wretched, ugly rampart, that emblem of human infirmity, of man's hopeless nastiness. And yet, despite the disfiguring insult of the Wall and the discord it embodies, Jerusalem remains proud and unbowed. It stands there still, nestled between the clement plain and the harsh Judean Desert, drawing the strength it needs for its survival from spiritual sources untapped by either the kings of yesteryear or the charlatans of today. Although cruelly outraged by injustice and suffering, the city continues to keep the faith—this evening, more than ever. It seems to be rapt in prayer amid its candles, as though it has regained all the force of its prophecies now that its people are preparing for sleep. Hopefully, it enters silence like a peaceful harbor. A breeze laden with incense and fragrance stirs the leaves in the garden. If only you listen closely, you can detect the pulse of the gods; if only you reach out your hand, you can gather in their mercy; if only you pay attention, you can be one with them.

I loved Jerusalem when I was a boy. Standing in front of the Wailing Wall, I felt the same thrill as I did before the Dome of the Rock, and I couldn't remain unmoved by the serenity emanating from the Church of the Holy Sepulcher. I moved from one part of the city to another as though turning from an Ashkenazi fable to a Bedouin tale, with equal delight, and I didn't need to be a conscientious objector to distrust policies requiring armed struggle and sermons based on hatred. Gazing upon Jerusalem's sacred structures was enough to persuade me to oppose everything that might injure their enduring grandeur. And still today, beneath its surface holiness, the city is like an odalisque longing for her lover, ready to burst into sensuous joy. It frowns unhappily upon the uproar of its citizens, hoping against hope that enlightenment may come and deliver their minds from their dark torment. By turns Olympus and ghetto, muse and concubine, temple and arena, Jerusalem suffers from an inability to inspire poems without enflaming passions. It's crumbling, heavyhearted, breaking up like its prayers amid the blasphemy of guns. . . .

"So how was it?" Kim asks, interrupting my reverie.

"What?"

"Your day."

I wipe my mouth on a napkin. "They didn't expect me to

show up there," I say. "Now that they've got me on their hands, they don't know what to do."

"You don't say," she replies. Then, after a pause: "And what's your plan, exactly?"

"I don't have one. Since I don't know where to start, I'm just diving right in."

She pours me some sparkling water. Her hand is not calm.

"You think they're going to let you do whatever you want?"

"I don't have the slightest idea."

"In that case, what do you propose to accomplish?"

"It's up to them to tell me that, Kim. I'm not a cop or an investigative journalist. I'm angry, and my anger would eat me alive if I didn't take some action. Frankly, I don't know exactly what I want. I'm obeying something that's inside me, guiding me wherever it chooses. I don't know where I'm going, and I don't care. But I can assure you that I already feel better now that I've stirred up the anthill a little. You should have seen their faces when they realized I was taking it to them. . . . Do you know what I mean?"

"Not really, Amin. Nothing good can come from this behavior of yours. In my opinion, you're looking for the wrong kind of guy. You need a shrink, not a sheikh. Those people don't have to account to you for anything."

"They killed my wife."

"Sihem killed *herself*," Kim says softly, as though she's afraid to wake up my demons. "She knew what she was doing; she'd chosen her destiny. It's not the same thing."

Kim's words exasperate me.

She takes my hand. "If you don't know what you want, why insist on going in blind? That must be the wrong move. Let's say these folks consent to a meeting with you; what then? What do you expect to get out of them? They'll tell you your wife died for the Great Cause and invite you to do the same. These are people who have renounced this world, Amin. Remember what Navid told you about them. They're martyrs in waiting, hot to get the green light so they can go up in smoke. I'm telling you, you're making a mistake. Let's go back home to Tel Aviv and let the police do their job."

I draw my hand back from under hers.

"I don't understand what's happening to me, Kim. I'm perfectly clearheaded, but I've got this incredible need to go my own way. I feel that I can't mourn for my wife until I look into the eyes of the son of a bitch who stole her mind. It's not a question of what I'm going to say to him or throw at him. That doesn't matter. I just want to see what he looks like. I want to understand what he's got that I don't. . . . It's hard to explain, Kim. So many ideas are buzzing around in my brain. Sometimes, I'm so filled with regret, I could die. Sometimes, Sihem seems like the worst slut in the world. I have to know which of us sinned against the other."

"And you think these people are going to give you the answer?"

"I don't know! I don't know anything!"

My shout reverberates in the silence like a detonation.

Kim sits paralyzed in her chair, holding a dishcloth against her mouth, her eyes wide.

I raise my hands to my shoulders to regain my self-control. "I apologize, Kim. Obviously, this is all too much for me. But you have to let me do what I want to do. If something happens to me, well, maybe that's just what I'm looking for."

"I'm worried about you."

"I don't doubt that for a second, Kim. More often than not, I feel ashamed for behaving this way, but I refuse to calm down. And the more anyone tries to reason with me, the less I feel like pulling myself together. Do you understand?"

Kim puts her dishcloth down without answering me. Her lips quiver for a long minute before they can catch up with their words. She takes a deep breath, turns her sorrowful eyes on me, and says, "I knew someone a long time ago. He was an ordinary boy, except that I was struck by him from the first time I saw him. He was loving and kind. I don't know how he did it, but before our romance was very old, he'd managed to become the center of my universe. Every time he smiled at me, it was like a bolt from the blue, and if he was angry at me, the whole world went dark. I loved him impossibly. Sometimes, at the height of my happiness, I would ask myself the terrible question, What if he leaves me? And all at once, I could see my soul separating from my body. Without him, I knew, it would be all over for me. And then one evening, without warning, he threw his things into a suitcase and walked out of my life. For years, I felt like empty skin after a molt—transparent and dangling in midair. Then, after a few more years passed, I realized I was still there, my soul and body were still together, and all at once, I recovered my spirits. . . ."

Her fingers squeeze mine, hard and tight.

"What I'm trying to say is simple, Amin. It's no good expecting the worst; it'll always surprise us. And if we're unlucky and we have to hit bottom, it's up to us, and to us alone, whether we stay down there or climb back up. But you have to know where to put your feet. It's very easy to slip. Move too fast, and you wind up back in the ditch. But is that the end of the world? I don't think so. Once you resign yourself, you're back on top."

There's a screeching of brakes as a car pulls up outside the apartment building. Doors slam, and the sound of footsteps drowns out the insects. Someone knocks on the door and then rings the bell. Kim opens the door to find the police, accompanied by the neighbor from apartment 38. The officer is a blond-haired man of a certain age, frail and courteous. Three agents are with him, all of them armed to the teeth. He apologizes for disturbing us and asks to see our papers. Closely followed by the policeman, we go to our respective rooms to get the documents in question.

The officer checks our identity cards and our professional IDs, lingering over mine. Then he says, "You're an Israeli citizen, Mr. Jaafari?"

"Do you have a problem with that?"

Irritated by my question, he looks me up and down, gives us back our papers, and addresses Kim: "You're Benjamin Yehuda's sister, ma'am?"

"Yes."

"Your brother's an old acquaintance of mine. Hasn't he come back from the United States yet?"

"He's in Tel Aviv. Preparing for a forum."

"That's right, I forgot. I've been told he had an operation recently. I hope he's feeling better now."

"Officer, my brother's never set foot in an operating room."

He nods, salutes her, and signs to his men to follow him outside. Before closing the door, we hear the neighbor from 38 declare that Benjamin never said anything to him about any sister. The car doors slam again, and the police vehicle pulls off with tires squealing.

"Confidence reigns," I say to Kim.

"And how!" she agrees, walking back to the table.

———

I don't close my eyes all night. Sometimes staring at the ceiling hard enough to crack it, sometimes sucking on the umpteenth cigarette, I chew over Kim's words until I've had enough of them, but I never find their taste. Kim doesn't understand me, and—what's worse—I'm not any farther along in that field of knowledge than she is. Nevertheless, I refuse to put up with any more lectures. The only thing I want to hear is what's already in my head, dragging me willy-nilly toward the only tunnel that offers a glimmer of light now that all the other exits are closed.

In the morning, very early, I sneak out of the flat while Kim's still sleeping, jump into a taxi, and head for Bethlehem. The Grand Mosque is nearly deserted. One of the faithful, occupied with ordering the books in a makeshift library, can't catch me in time. I dash across the prayer hall, lift the curtain behind the *minbar*, and burst into a plain, unadorned room, where a young man dressed in a white *kamis* and wearing a cap is reading the Qur'an. He's sitting cross-legged on a cushion in front of a low table. The assistant charges in behind me and grabs my shoulder; I push him away and confront the imam. Though he's clearly outraged by my intrusion, he tells his disciple to return to his post. The man grumbles and withdraws. The imam closes his book and glares at me angrily.

"This isn't a barn," he says.

"I'm sorry, but it was the only way to see you."

"That's not a reason."

"I need to speak with you."

"On what subject?"

"I'm Dr.—"

"I know who you are. I'm the one who gave the order to keep you away from the mosque. I don't know what you hope to find in Bethlehem, and I don't think your presence in our community is a good idea."

He places the Qur'an on a tiny stand and rises to his feet. He's small and ascetic, but his being vibrates with boundless energy and resolve.

His impressively black eyes weigh on mine.

He says, "You're not welcome among us, Dr. Jaafari. Nor do you have the right to enter this sanctuary without performing the proper ablutions and without taking off

your shoes." As he adds this last bit, he wipes the corners
of his mouth with one finger. "Even though you're losing
your mind, you might at least retain some semblance of decency. This is a place of prayer. And we know that you're a
recalcitrant believer—practically a renegade—that you
don't follow the path of your ancestors nor conform to
their principles, and that you have long since dissociated
yourself from their Cause by opting for another nationality.
Am I mistaken?"

His response to my silence is a grimace, heavy with dis-
dain. Then he declares in a sententious voice, "In that case,
I fail to see what we can talk about."

"About my wife!"

"She's dead," he replies coldly.

"But I haven't mourned for her yet."

"That's your problem, Doctor."

The curtness of his tone, together with his summary
manner, unsettles me. I can't believe that a man thought to
be so close to God can be so far from men, so insensitive to
their distress.

"I don't like the way you talk to me."

"There's a vast number of things you don't like, Doctor,
but in my opinion, that fact does not exempt you from anything at all. I don't know who had charge of your education, but of one thing I'm certain: You went to the wrong
school. Furthermore, nothing authorizes you to put on this
air of outrage or to place yourself above ordinary mortals—
not your social success, and not your wife's brave deed,
which, by the way, doesn't raise you a whit in our esteem.

To me, you're nothing but a poor orphan, without faith and without salvation, wandering around like a sleepwalker in broad daylight. Even if you could walk on water, you couldn't erase the insult that you represent. For the real bastard isn't the man who doesn't know his father; it's the man who doesn't know his tradition. Of all the black sheep, he's the most to be pitied and the least to be lamented."

He sizes me up as though trying to decide where to bite me. "Now go away," he says. "You bring the evil eye upon our dwelling place."

"I forbid you—"

"Get out!"

He stretches out his arm like a blade, pointing to the curtain.

"One more thing, Doctor. Remember, the margin between assimilation and disintegration is quite narrow. There's not much room for maneuver."

"You're a crackpot!" I cry.

"I am enlightened," he replies, correcting me.

"You think you've been charged with a divine mission."

"Every brave man is charged with one. The man who isn't is only conceited, selfish, and unjust."

He claps his hands. His disciple, who has clearly been listening at the door, comes in and seizes me by the shoulder again. I push him away violently and turn back to the imam. "I'm not leaving Bethlehem before I talk to a leader of your movement."

"Please get out of my house," he says, picking up his Qur'an from its stand.

He sits back down on his cushion and acts as though I'm no longer here.

———

Kim calls me on my mobile phone. She's quite exercised about the way I gave her the slip. By way of making it up to her, I agree to let her join me in Bethlehem and arrange to meet her in a service station at the entrance to the town. From there, we go to my foster sister's house.

Leila has yet to recover from her most recent relapse. Convinced that the imam's men are going to be watching the house, Kim and I remain at her bedside. Yasser joins us a little later. He finds Kim in the act of caring for his wife and doesn't try to find out whether she's a friend of mine or a physician making an emergency call. Yasser and I go into another room for a chat. By way of preventing me from spoiling his day, he enumerates at some length the dangers threatening his press and deplores his mounting debts and the way his creditors are blackmailing him. I listen to him until he runs out of breath and it's my turn. I tell him about my brief interview with the imam. Yasser contents himself with shaking his chin, while a deep wrinkle forms on his forehead. He's too prudent to risk any comment, but he's gravely disturbed to hear about the imam's attitude toward me.

It's evening now, and since nothing or nobody has turned up, I decide to go back to the mosque. Two men jump me in an alleyway. The first one grabs me by the collar and kicks my feet out from under me; the second rams his knee into my hip before I hit the ground. I wedge my injured wrist into my armpit, cover my face with my arms, and curl up to protect myself from the blows raining down on me from every side. In between kicks and punches, the two promise to lynch me on the spot if they find me prowling around these parts again. I try to get up or drag myself into a doorway; they haul me by my ankles into the middle of the street and flail away at my back and my legs. The few rubbernecks who appear beat an immediate retreat, leaving me to the fury of my attackers. In the midst of contortions and outcries, something explodes in my head, and I lose consciousness. . . .

When I come to, I'm surrounded by a bunch of little kids. One of them asks whether I'm dead; another replies that I'm probably drunk. When I sit up, they all jump back and run away from me.

Night has fallen. I stagger along, leaning on walls, with wobbly knees and a loud buzz in my head. I have to perform several acrobatic feats before I can reach my brother-in-law's house.

"My God!" Kim screams.

Aided by Yasser, she places me on a padded bench and starts unbuttoning my shirt. She's relieved when she discovers only cuts and bruises; my body bears no wound from blade or firearm. After giving me first aid, she picks up the telephone to call the police, causing Yasser to suffer what looks like a heart attack. I tell Kim that calling the cops is out of the question; I have no intention of backing off, especially after the thrashing I've just received. She protests, calls me a madman, and begs me to go back to Jerusalem with her at once. I categorically refuse to leave Bethlehem. Kim sees that I'm totally blinded by hatred, and that nothing will make me give up my fixed purpose.

The next day, aching all over and dragging one foot, I go back to the mosque. No one comes to throw me out. Some of the faithful, seeing that I don't rise for the prayer, assume that I'm a mental defective.

In the evening, a caller telephones Yasser's house to say that someone will come to pick me up in half an hour. Kim warns me that it's surely a trap; I say I don't care. I'm tired of defying the devil and getting nothing but a few blows in return; I want to see him whole, even if doing so means I have to suffer for the rest of my life.

To begin with, a young boy comes to fetch me at Yasser's. He asks me to follow him to the square, where a teenager takes charge of me. This lad leads me on a long walk through a working-class suburb plunged in darkness; I suspect he's going in circles in order to throw me off. At last, we reach a rickety little shop. A man is waiting for us, standing beside a metal shutter pulled halfway down. He dismisses the teenager and invites me to follow him inside the building. At the end of a corridor littered with empty crates and burst cartons, I'm turned over to a second man. He and I cross a small courtyard and step into a poorly lighted patio. We enter a bare room, where he asks me to undress and change into a jogging outfit and a pair of new espadrilles. He explains that these are security measures taken in case the Shin Bet have planted a bug on me, a transmitter that could identify my exact position at any given moment. The man also uses this opportunity to make sure I'm not wearing a wire or any other sort of gadget. An hour later, a small van comes to pick me up. I'm blindfolded and made to lie down on the floor of the van. After many turnings, we come to a stop and I hear a door or gate creak and then slam shut behind the vehicle. A dog begins to bark, only to be silenced at once by a few gruff words. Arms lift me out of the van, hands remove my blindfold. I'm in a large courtyard, at one end of which motionless armed silhouettes are standing. For a moment, a prickly chill runs down my spine, and suddenly I'm afraid; I feel I've been caught like a rat in a trap.

The driver of the van seizes my elbow and pushes me toward a house on my right. He doesn't accompany me very far. A tall fellow who looks like a circus strongman ushers me into a drawing room covered with a deep-pile carpet, where a young man in a black *kamis* with embroidered collar and sleeves opens his arms to receive me. "Brother Amin, it's a privilege to welcome you to my humble dwelling," he says with a slight Lebanese accent.

His face tells me nothing. I don't think I've seen or met him before. He's a handsome man, with bright eyes and fine features spoiled by a mustache too thick to be real; he can't be more than thirty.

He comes up to me and embraces me, patting my back in the mujahideen way.

"Brother Amin, my friend, my destiny. You cannot imagine how honored I am."

I figure it's no use reminding him of the great thumping his gorillas gave me last night.

"Come," he says, taking my hand. "Have a seat."

I stare at the colossus standing guard beside the door. With an imperceptible nod, my host dismisses him.

"I'm very sorry about yesterday," he declares, "but you have to admit you asked for it, in a way."

"If that's the price to pay for a meeting with you, I find the charge rather high."

He laughs.

"Others before you have not gotten off so cheaply," he confides to me with a hint of arrogance. "We're going through a period when nothing can be left to chance. The slightest laxity, and everything could come crashing down."

He hikes up the skirts of his *kamis* and sits down cross-legged upon a mat.

"Your loss moves me to the bottom of my soul, brother Amin. As God is my witness, I am suffering as much as you."

"I doubt it. These are things that can't be shared equally."

"I, too, have lost loved ones."

"I haven't suffered their loss as you have."

He presses his lips together. "I see."

"I'm not here on a courtesy call," I say to him.

"I know. What can I do for you?"

"My wife is dead. But before she went and blew herself

up in the middle of a bunch of schoolchildren, she came to this town to meet her mentor." As I speak, rage floods over me like a dark, uncontainable tide, and I add, "It makes me very angry to think that she preferred a set of fundamentalists to me. And my anger doubles when I consider how I was taken in. I admit I'm more furious about not having seen anything coming than I am about all the rest. My wife was an Islamist? Since when, pray tell? I can't get this through my head. She was a woman of her time. She liked to travel, she liked to swim, she liked sipping her lemonade on the terraces outside the shops, and she was too proud of her hair to hide it under a head scarf. What tales did you tell her? How did you make a monster, a terrorist, a suicidal fundamentalist out of a woman who couldn't bear to hear a puppy whine?"

He's disappointed. His charm offensive, which he must have worked on for hours before receiving my visit, seems to be foundering. This isn't the reaction he expected. He was hoping I'd be so impressed by all the fantastic rigmarole I had to go through to get here, including my consensual "kidnapping," that I'd be put in a weak position. I myself don't understand where this aggressive insolence of mine is coming from. It makes my hands shake, but it doesn't crack my voice; it makes my heart beat faster, but it doesn't bend my knees. Caught in a vise between the precariousness of my situation and the rage aroused in me by my host's haughty zeal and tacky costume, I choose the reckless option. I need to show this operetta chieftain in no uncertain terms that I'm not afraid of him. I need to throw in his face the loathing and the venom that fanatics of his kind produce in me.

For a long time, the commander kneads his fingers, unsure of where to start.

At last, with a sigh, he says, "I don't appreciate the brutality of your reprimands, brother Amin. But I put that down to the intensity of your grief."

"You can put it wherever you please."

His face turns red. "I beg you to refrain from crudeness. I will not tolerate it. Particularly when it comes from the mouth of an eminent surgeon. I have agreed to receive you for one simple reason: so that I can explain to you, once and for all, why making a spectacle of yourself in our town is an exercise in futility. There's nothing for you here. You wanted to meet a leader of our movement. Well, the thing is done. Now you're going to go back to Tel Aviv and put this interview behind you. I wish to tell you, furthermore, that I did not personally know your wife. She was not acting under our banner, but we appreciate what she did."

He lifts his burning eyes to mine. "And one last remark, Doctor. By dint of trying to resemble your adopted brothers, you've lost all discernment when it comes to your own. An Islamist is a political activist. He has but one ambition: to establish a theocratic state in his country and take full advantage of its sovereignty and its independence. A fundamentalist is an extremist *jihadi*. He believes neither in the sovereignty of Muslim states nor in their autonomy. In his view, these are vassal states that will be called upon to dissolve themselves and form the one, sole Caliphate. The fundamentalist dreams of a single, indivisible *umma*, the great Muslim community that will extend from Indonesia to Morocco, and which, if it cannot convert the West to Islam, will subjugate or destroy it. We're not Islamists, Dr. Jaafari, and we're not fundamentalists, either. We are only the children of a ravaged, despised people, fighting with whatever means we can to recover our homeland and our dignity. Nothing more, nothing less."

He considers me for a few moments to see whether I've taken all this in; then, returning to the contemplation of his immaculate fingernails, he goes on: "I never met your wife, and I'm sorry for that. She deserved that we should kiss her feet. What she offered us, with her sacrifice, gives us comfort and instruction. I understand why you feel dazed and bewildered. It's because you haven't yet realized the scope of what your wife accomplished. At the moment, your pride as a husband has been wounded, but one day, the wound will heal and you'll be able to see further and more clearly. The fact that your wife told you nothing of the combat she was engaged in does not signify that she betrayed you. She simply had nothing to tell you, she had no account to give to anyone, because she had put herself in God's hands. I'm not asking you to forgive her— what's a husband's forgiveness to one who has received the Lord's grace? I'm asking you to turn the page. The tale goes on."

"I want to know why," I say stupidly.

"Why what? That was her affair; it's a matter that doesn't concern you."

"I was her husband."

"She was aware of that. If she didn't want to confide in you, she must have had her reasons. And by keeping quiet, she disqualified you."

"Bullshit! She had obligations toward me. A wife can't deceive her husband like that. Not this husband, in any case. I never wronged her in any way. And it was my life she blew into smithereens, too, not just hers. My life and the lives of seventeen people she'd never met. And you ask me why I want to know? Well, I want to know *everything*. I want to know the whole truth."

"Which truth? Hers or yours? The truth of a woman who realized where her duty lay, or the truth of a man who believes you need only turn your back on a tragedy to wash your hands of it? Whose truth do you want to know, *Dr. Amin Jaafari*? The truth of a Bedouin who thinks he's free and clear because he's got an Israeli passport? The truth of the serviceable Arab par excellence who's honored wherever he goes, who gets invited to fancy parties by people who want to show how tolerant and considerate they are? The truth of someone who thinks he can change sides like changing a shirt, with no trace left behind? Is that the truth you're looking for, or is it the one you're running away from? What planet do you live on, *sir*? We're in a world where people tear one another to pieces every day that God sends. We spend our evenings gathering our dead and our mornings burying them. Our homeland is violated right and left, our children can't remember what the word *school* means, and our daughters have no more dreams, because their Prince Charmings choose to court the Intifada instead. Our cities are being buried by machines on caterpillar tracks, our patron saints don't know which way to turn, and you, simply because you're nice and warm in your golden cage, refuse to see the inferno consuming us. It's your right, after all. Everyone steers his ship as he thinks fit. But please don't come here asking questions about those who are sickened by your apathy and your selfishness and do not hesitate to give their lives to wake you up. Your wife died for *your* redemption, Mr. Jaafari."

"You talk about redemption?" I say. "You're the one who needs it. You dare to talk to me about selfishness when you've taken away the creature I cherished most in the world? You dare to feed me these tales of courage and dignity when you remain at your ease in your little corner and send women and kids to do your dirty work? Get it straight: We do indeed live on the same planet, *my brother*, but we're not staying at the same address. You have chosen to kill; I have chosen to save. Where you see an enemy, I see a patient. I'm neither selfish nor indifferent, and I've got as much self-esteem as anyone. I just want to be able to live my share of existence without being obliged to detract from the existence of others. I don't believe in prophecies that favor suffering over common sense. I came naked into the world, I'll leave it naked, what I possess doesn't belong to me, and neither do other people's lives. All human unhappiness comes from this misunderstanding. You have to be prepared to give back what God has loaned you. No earthly thing belongs to you, not really. Neither the homeland you talk about nor the grave where you'll be dust among the dust."

My finger won't stop jabbing at him. The commander doesn't flinch. He hears me out to the end, his eyes on his fingernails, without deigning to wipe the drops of my saliva off his face.

After a long silence that seems interminable, he raises an eyebrow slightly and takes a deep breath before finally turning his eyes back to me.

"I'm stunned by what I've just heard, Amin. It breaks my heart and pierces my soul. However great your grief, it doesn't give you the right to blaspheme in this way. You talk to me about your wife, and you don't hear me talk to you about your country. You may refuse to have one, but you can't force others to renounce theirs. And those who clamor for a nation of their own are offering up their lives in its Cause, every day and every night. Not for them this dying by degrees, disdained by others and contemptuous of themselves. In their view, there's either decency or death, either freedom or the grave, either dignity or a tomb. And no loss, no bereavement will stop them from fighting for their honor, which they rightly see as essential to existence. *'Blessedness is not the reward of virtue, but is virtue itself.'* "

He claps his hands. The door opens, revealing the colossus. The conversation is over.

Before dismissing me, the commander speaks again: "I'm very sorry for you, Dr. Amin Jaafari. Obviously, we haven't chosen the same road. We could spend months and years striving for mutual understanding, and neither of us would ever be willing to listen to the other. So there's no point in continuing. Go back home. We have no more to say to each other, you and I."

12.

Kim was right: I should have turned the letter over to Navid. He would have made better use of it than I have. Nor was she wrong when she warned me against myself— of all the improbabilities, it turns out that I myself was the hardest to account for. It took me some time to face the facts. I've been incredibly lucky to get this far in one piece—empty-handed, of course, and not completely un-scathed, but still on my feet. The failure of this adventure will pursue me for a long time, as persistent as a moral dilemma, as vile as a practical joke. What did I get out of it, when all is said and done? All I did was circle around an illusion like a moth around a flame, more obsessed by my own curiosity than fascinated by the candle's deadly light. The trapdoor I wore myself out trying to wrest open didn't yield any of its secrets; in the end, all I got was a faceful of stale air and spiderwebs.

I no longer feel the need to go any further.

Now that I've seen with my own eyes what a war leader and creator of suicide bombers looks like, my demons have loosened their grip on me. I've decided to shut down this traveling circus of mine and return to Tel Aviv.

Kim's relieved. She's driving in silence, grasping the steering wheel with both hands as though trying to assure herself that this is no hallucination, that she's actually bringing me back home. Ever since this morning, she hasn't uttered a word—she's afraid she'll make some blunder and I'll change my mind all of a sudden. She got up before dawn, packed the bags and the car without a sound, and didn't wake me up until most of our stuff was in the trunk and ready to go.

We leave the Jewish areas with our eyes straight ahead, as though we were wearing blinders. Don't think about looking left or right or stopping for any reason at all; the smallest inadvertence could make everything go wrong. Kim stares at the street in front of us and makes a beeline for the nearest exit from the city. The torments of the night are over; the dawn promises a radiant day. The immaculate sky, still heavy from its guiltless sleep, awakens with a lazy stretch. The city seems to be having trouble getting out of bed. A few furtive early risers emerge from the darkness, hugging the walls like shadow puppets, their eyes swollen with aborted dreams. There are a few sudden noises: someone raising a metal shutter, someone else starting a vehicle. A bus belches crudely as it returns to its terminal. In Jerusalem, people are very cautious in the morning, out of superstition: The first words and deeds at dawn, it's said, usually shape the rest of the day.

Kim takes advantage of the smoothly flowing traffic to drive fast—very fast. She doesn't realize how nervous she is. I'd say she's trying to outrun my mood swings; she doesn't want me to have a change of heart and decide to go back to Bethlehem.

She doesn't straighten her back until the last suburbs of the city are disappearing in the rearview mirror.

"Where's the fire?" I say.

She takes her foot off the accelerator as though she's suddenly realized she's treading on a snake. In reality, it's my broken voice that particularly bothers her. I feel so tired, so wretched. What did I go looking for in Bethlehem? A few lies to spruce up what's left of my image? A modicum of dignity at a time when nothing's going right? Did I want to display my rage in a public place so the sons of bitches who've lanced my dream like an abscess can know how much I despise them? Suppose everyone felt compassion for my grief and my revulsion; suppose people stepped out of my way and bowed to me when I looked at them—what then? What would that change? What wound would be cauterized; what fracture would be set? Deep inside, I'm not completely sure I want to dig all the way down to the roots of my misfortune. I'm certainly not afraid of conflict, but how do you cross swords with ghosts? It's just too bloody obvious that I'm not up to the job. I don't know a thing about gurus and their henchmen. All my life, I've stubbornly turned my back on leaders' diatribes and the activities of their zealous followers, and I've clung to my ambitions like a jockey to his horse. I renounced my tribe, agreed to leave my mother's side, made concession after concession in order to dedicate myself to my career alone; I didn't have time to take an interest in the traumatic events that undermined hopes for reconciliation between two chosen peoples who have elected to turn a land blessed by God into a field of horror and rage. I don't remember ever applauding the combatants on one side or condemning the combatants on the other; they all share an attitude I find senseless and depressing. I have never felt implicated in any way at all in this bloody conflict, which is in reality just a slugfest at close quarters between the punching bags and the scapegoats of history, villainous as it is, and always ready to repeat itself. I've encountered a great deal of contemptuous hostility, and I've learned that the only way to keep from resembling those who demonstrate it is not to act as they do. Instead of turning the other cheek or fighting back, I chose to care for patients. I practice the noblest of all human professions, and nothing can make me compromise the pride I take in it. My visit to Bethlehem was nothing but a reflexive plunge; my pseudo courage was only a diversion. Who am I to think I can triumph where trained professionals run into brick walls every day? I'm up against a perfectly well-oiled organization, seasoned by years of cabals and armed exploits, that manages to elude the secret police's most accomplished sleuths. All I have on my side are my frustrations—the frustrations of a husband who's been cheated on—and a hyperventilating fury without any real clout. There's a duel going on, with no place for qualms and even less for emotion; only guns, exploding belts, and counterthrusts carry any weight, and woe to the ventriloquists whose puppets seize up. It's a duel without pity and without rules, where hesitations are fatal and mistakes irreparable, where the end generates its own means, and where salvation is not much thought of, having been largely supplanted by the exaltations of revenge and spectacular death. Now, I've always felt a holy terror for tanks and bombs, and I've never seen anything in them but the most complete expression of the worst traits of humankind. I have nothing to do with the world I desecrated in Bethlehem; I don't know its rituals, I'm ignorant of its requirements, and I don't think I'm fit for learning much about them. I hate wars and revolutions and these dramas of redemptive violence that turn upon themselves like endlessly long screws and haul entire generations through the same murderous absurdities, apparently without ERROR signals going off in anybody's head. I'm a surgeon: In my view, there's enough suffering inherent in human flesh, and no need for healthy people to inflict more on one another every chance they get.

When the buildings of Tel Aviv start shimmering in the distance, I say to Kim, "Drop me off at my house."

"You've got some stuff to pick up?"

"No, I just want to go home."

She furrows her brow. "It's too soon."

"It's my house, Kim. I have to go back there sooner or later."

Kim realizes she's made a mistake. With a gesture of irritation, she flips some strands of hair out of her eyes. "That wasn't what I meant, Amin."

"No harm done."

Kim bites her lips as we roll through the next quarter of a mile. Then she says, "It's still that damned 'sign' you weren't able to decipher, isn't it?"

I don't answer her question.

A tractor bounds down the side of a hill. The boy at the wheel has to hold on tightly to keep his seat. Two red dogs escort him, one on each side of his machine; one keeps its nose to the ground, while the other looks distracted. A small worm-eaten wooden house comes into view from behind a hedge before a cluster of trees makes it disappear as if by magic. Once again, the fields take up their headlong march across the plain; the coming season looks very promising.

Kim waits until she passes a military convoy before she returns to the charge: "Didn't you feel comfortable in my house?"

I turn toward her; she keeps her eyes straight ahead. I say, "If I hadn't been comfortable, I wouldn't have stayed, Kim, as you know very well. I appreciate the fact that you're by my side. But I need to step back a little and think about the last few days at my leisure."

Kim's chiefly worried that I might do myself harm, that I won't be able to bear an interview with myself, that I'll give in to my torment in the end. She thinks I'm on the verge of total depression and capable of taking an irreversible step. She doesn't have to declare any of this—everything about her betrays her deep anxiety: her fingers, drumming on whatever surface they encounter; her lips, which can form only grimaces; her eyes, which dart away whenever mine become insistent; her throat, which she has to clear every time she's got something to say to me. I wonder how she manages to maintain her focus and keep me under such steady vigilance.

"All right," she says. "I'll drop you off at your house and come by to pick you up this evening. We'll have dinner at my place."

Her voice sounds uncomfortable.

I wait patiently until she turns toward me and then I say, "I need to be alone for a little while."

She pretends to consider that. Then her mouth twists and she asks, "Until when?"

"Until everything settles down."

"That could take a while."

"I'm not so far gone," I say to reassure her. "I just need to clear my mind."

"Very well," she says with a hint of badly disguised anger.

After a long silence, she says, "Can I at least come by and see you?"

"I'll call you up as soon as that's possible."

Since she's oversensitive, this statement comes as a blow to her.

"Don't take it so hard, Kim," I say. "This isn't about you. I know, it's hard for me to justify, but you know perfectly well what I'm trying to say."

"I don't want you to isolate yourself, that's all. I don't believe you're ready yet to recover on your own. And I don't feel like chewing off what's left of my fingers."

"I hope you don't."

"Why not let Professor Menach examine you? He's an eminent shrink and a friend of yours to boot."

"I'll go and see him, I promise, but not in my present state. I need to reconstruct myself by myself first. Then I'll be in the proper condition for hearing what he's got to say."

She drops me off at my house, not daring to accompany me inside. Before I close the gate, I smile at her. She gives me a sad wink.

"Try not to let your 'sign' ruin your life, Amin. In the long run, looking for it is going to wear you out, and afterward you won't be able to get ahold of yourself again. You'll disintegrate like a rotten mummy."

Without waiting for me to react, she drives off.

When the sound of Kim's Nissan dies away and I find myself facing my house and its silence, I realize the extent of my solitude; I miss Kim already. I'm alone again. "I don't like leaving you alone," Sihem told me the evening before she left for Kafr Kanna. And all at once, everything comes back to me—at the moment when I least expect it. Sihem prepared a meal fit for a king that evening, didn't she? All my favorite dishes. We had a candlelight dinner in the living room, just the two of us. She didn't eat much. She contented herself with picking delicately at her plate. She was so beautiful, and at the same time so distant. "Why are you sad, my love?" I asked her. "I don't like leaving you alone, darling," she replied. "Three days, that's not so long," I said. And she declared, "To me, it's an eternity." That was it; that was her message, *the sign I wasn't able to decipher.* But how could I have imagined the abyss behind her bright eyes? That night she gave herself to me as she had never done before. How could I have perceived the farewell behind so much generosity?

I tremble on my threshold for a while before I cross it.

The housekeeper still hasn't been here. I try to reach her by telephone a few times, but I keep getting her answering machine. I decide to take matters into my own hands. The house is as Captain Moshé's men left it: rooms turned upside down, drawers spilled onto the floor and their contents scattered, wardrobes emptied out, bookcases capsized, furniture moved about and sometimes overturned. Since I've been here, dust and dead leaves have invaded the place, thanks to the broken panes of glass and the windows I forgot to close. The yard is disgraceful—it's covered with beer cans, newspapers, and various other objects that my assailants from the other day left behind. I call up a glazier I know; he tells me he's on a job at the moment but promises to pass by before nightfall. I start putting the rooms back into some semblance of order: I pick up what's on the floor, replace the bookshelves and the drawers, separate damaged items from undamaged ones. When the glazier arrives, I'm just finishing with the sweeping. He helps me carry out the garbage bags and then goes to have a look at my windows while I withdraw to the kitchen for a smoke and a cup of coffee. He appears again with a notepad on which he's written down the various repair operations he'll have to carry out.

"Hurricane or vandalism?" he asks me.

I offer him a cup of coffee, which he gladly accepts. He's

a fat redhead with freckles all over his face, which is dominated by his large mouth; he's got round, flabby shoulders
and short legs ending in a pair of scuffed and slashed military boots. I've known him for years, and I've operated on
his father twice.

"There's a lot of work to do," he informs me. "Twenty-
three panes have to be replaced. You should also call a carpenter—you've got broken wood on two windows and
several shutters that need repair."

"You know a good carpenter?"

He squints as he considers this question. "There's one
who's not bad, but I'll have to find out if he's available on
short notice. As for me, I'll start tomorrow. I worked hard
all day today, and I'm wasted, so I'm just going to give you
an estimate this evening. Is that okay?"

I look at my watch. "All right," I say. "Tomorrow it is."

The glazier finishes his coffee with one gulp, stuffs his
notepad into a leather briefcase with worn-out straps, and
leaves. Since he seemed to know who trashed the house, I
was afraid he was going to bring up the attack, but he did
nothing of the kind. He noted down what he had to do and
that was all. I find him admirable.

After he drives off, I take a shower and go down to the
city. First a taxi drops me off at the garage where I parked
my car before I left for Jerusalem, and then I plant myself
behind my steering wheel and head for the seafront. The
frantic traffic forces me to turn into a parking area facing
the Mediterranean. Couples and families are tranquilly
strolling along the esplanades. I have dinner in a discreet lit-

tle restaurant, drink a couple of beers in a bar at the other end of the street, and then I go and loiter on the beach until the small hours of the night. The sound of the waves fills me with a kind of bliss. I return home a bit tipsy, but I've cleared my mind of a whole lot of dross.

I fall asleep in the armchair, fully dressed, my shoes still on my feet—sleep snatches me away between two puffs on a cigarette. The banging of a window awakens me with a start. I'm drenched with sweat. I think I must have had a bad dream, but it's impossible for me to remember just what it was about. I stand up, tottering. My heart leaps into my throat; shivers course up and down my back. I hear myself cry out, *"Who's there?"* I turn on the lights in the front hall, in the kitchen, in the bedrooms, ears cocked for a suspicious noise. *"Who's there?"* There's a French window open upstairs; its curtain billows in the wind. There's nobody on the balcony. I close the shutters and go back into the living room. But the presence remains, vague and near at the same time. My shivering intensifies. No doubt it's Sihem come back, or her ghost, or maybe even both of them. . . . Sihem . . . Gradually, she fills the space around me. By the end of a few palpitations, the whole place is replete with her, as full as an egg, leaving me only a tiny pocket of air so I won't suffocate. The mistress of the house pervades it again, all of it: the chandeliers, the chests of drawers, the curtains, the consoles, the colors. She's the one who chose the pictures, and she's the one who hung them on the walls. I can still see her backing up a few steps, a finger to her chin, leaning her head left and right to be sure the frame is straight. Sihem had a keen eye for detail. She left nothing to chance and could spend hours deliberating with herself about the placement of a painting or the fold of a curtain. I move from one part of the house to another, from the living room to the kitchen, and I feel as though I'm following her trail. My memories give way to scenes that are practically real. Sihem relaxes on the leather sofa, applying thin layers of pink polish to her fingernails. Every corner retains a piece of her shadow; every mirror reflects a bright fragment of her image; every rustling sound speaks of her. All I have to do is reach out my hand to gather up a laugh, a sigh, a waft of her perfume. "I want you to give me a daughter," I told her in the early days of our love. "Blond or brunette?" she replied, blushing. "I want her to be healthy and beautiful. I don't care much about the color of her hair or her eyes. I'd like her to have your features and your dimples, so that when she smiles, she'll be the spitting image of you."

I enter the upstairs sitting room, with its dark red velvet drapery, its milky white curtains on the windows, and its two imposing armchairs standing in the middle of a handsome Persian rug and facing a glass and chrome coffee table. One wall of the room is taken up from one end to the other by a huge cherrywood bookcase, filled with carefully ordered books and various ornaments brought home from distant lands. This room was our ivory tower, Sihem's and mine. No one else was ever admitted here. It was our intimate corner, our golden refuge. Sometimes we'd come here to commune with our silence and reactivate our senses, dulled and blunted by the noises of every day. We'd bring a

book or put on some music, and then we were off. We read
Kafka as well as Kahlil Gibran, and listened to Oum
Kalthoum and Pavarotti with the same gratitude. . . . All at
once, the hairs on my body bristle from head to feet. I feel
her breath in the hollow of my neck, heavy, warm, panting.
I know that all I have to do is turn around slightly and I'll
be face-to-face with her. I'll stand in the wild dance of the
waves emanating from her; I'll see her radiance, her immense eyes, more beautiful than in my maddest dreams. . . .

I don't turn around.

I back out of the sitting room until a draft of air dissipates her breath. In the bedroom, I switch on all the lamps
and all the ceiling lights to banish any trace of shadow. I
undress, smoke a last cigarette, swallow two tranquilizers,
and slip into bed.

Without turning off the lights.

———

The following morning, I'm surprised to find myself in the
upstairs sitting room with my face pressed to the window,
watching the sun come up. How did I make my way back to
this haunted spot? Of my own free will, or sleepwalking? I
have no idea.

The sky over Tel Aviv outdoes itself; there's not a hint of
cloud in sight. The moon has been reduced to a faint sliver.
The night's last stars fade out slowly in the opalescence of
the rising sun. On the other side of the gate, my neighbor
from across the street is cleaning the windshield of his car.

He's always the first one up in the neighborhood. As the manager of one of the most elegant restaurants in town, he insists on arriving at the big wholesale market before his competitors. Sometimes we've exchanged standard greetings in the darkness, when he was getting ready to go to the market and I was coming home from the hospital. Since the attack, he acts as though I don't exist.

Around nine o'clock, the glazier arrives in a sun-bleached van. Assisted by two pimply boys, he unloads his equipment and his sheets of glass with the meticulous care of a craftsman. He informs me that the carpenter will be here soon. And indeed, this latter individual shows up a few moments later, driving a pickup truck covered with a tarpaulin. He's a tall, withered fellow stuffed into threadbare overalls, his face deeply lined and his eyes deadly serious. He asks to see the damaged windows, and the glazier takes charge of showing him what has to be done. I stay on the bottom floor, sitting in an armchair, smoking and drinking coffee. For a moment, I think about stretching my legs and relaxing my mind in a little park not far from my house. It's a fine day—the sun is gilding the trees all around—but the risk that disagreeable encounters on the street may ruin my day dissuades me.

It's nearly eleven o'clock when Navid Ronnen calls me on the telephone. By this point, the carpenter has carried off the broken windows, which he has to repair in his shop. As for the glazier, he and his two assistants are still working upstairs, so silently that you'd think they were hiding.

"What's going on with you, old pal?" Navid asks, pleased

that he's finally got me on the other end of the line. "Are you an amnesia victim? Or just absentminded? You go away, you come back, you appear and reappear, and not once do you think about calling your good friend and giving him your address and phone number."

"Which ones? You yourself have just declared that I can't stay in one place."

He laughs.

"That's not an impediment. I'm pretty restless myself, but my wife knows exactly how to reach me when she wants to score a point. Did everything go all right in Jerusalem?"

"How do you know I was in Jerusalem?"

"I'm a cop," he says. Then, after a little laugh: "I called Kim, and Benjamin answered. He told me where you two had gone."

"Who told you I was back?"

"I called Benjamin, and Kim answered. How's that? Good enough? I'm calling because Margaret really wants you to come over for dinner. It's been forever since she's seen you."

"Not this evening, Navid. I've got some work to do on the house. There's a team of glaziers over here right now. The carpenter came this morning."

"So we'll make it tomorrow."

"I don't know if I'll be finished here by then."

Navid clears his throat, thinks a bit, and then makes an offer: "If your house needs a lot of work, I can send someone to help you."

"No, they're all small repair jobs. I've got enough people over here already."

Navid clears his throat again. This is a tic that manifests itself whenever he's embarrassed. "But surely they're not going to spend the night there?"

"No, but it seems like it. Thanks for the call, and love to Margaret."

Since it's noon and Kim has given no sign of herself, I believe she must have gone to Navid and asked him to call and determine whether or not I was still among the living.

The carpenter brings back my windows, installs them by himself, and checks to see that they're functioning properly as I look on. He has me sign an invoice, puts my money in his pocket, and withdraws, an extinguished cigarette butt stuck in the corner of his mouth. The glazier and his assistants have been gone for a good while. I've got my house back again; I recognize its calmness—the peace of the convalescent—and its mysterious shadows. I go upstairs to the sitting room to tempt my ghosts. Nothing's moving in the corners. I sink into a large chair facing a newly repaired window and watch night come down over the city like a cleaver, bloodying the horizon.

Sihem smiles from a framed photograph on top of the stereo system. One eye looks larger than the other, probably because of her forced smile. You always smile for the photographer when he's persuasive enough, even if your heart's not in it. This is an old photograph, one of the very first ones taken after we got married. I remember that it was for her passport. Sihem didn't really have her heart set on taking a honeymoon trip. She knew my resources were limited and preferred investing in a less dreary apartment than the one we had in the suburbs.

I get up and take a closer look at the photograph. To my left, on a shelf otherwise loaded with compact discs, there's a leather-bound photo album. Almost mechanically, I pick it up, go back to my chair, and start leafing through the album. I don't feel any particular emotion. It's as though I were flipping through a magazine while waiting my turn in a dentist's office. The photographs pass in review, captives of the instant in which they were taken, cold as the glazed paper on which they reveal themselves, stripped of any affective charge capable of moving me: Sihem under a beach umbrella, her face masked by an enormous pair of sunglasses, at Sharm-el-Sheikh; Sihem on the Champs-Elysées in Paris; the two of us posing alongside one of Her Britannic Majesty's guards; in the yard with my nephew Adel; at a party; at a reception in my honor; with her grandmother on the farm in Kafr Kanna; her uncle Abbas, with rubber boots and muddy knees; Sihem in front of the mosque in the Nazareth neighborhood where she was born. . . . I keep browsing, passing over memories without lingering on them very much. It's as if I were turning the pages of a former life, of a closed case. Then one of the snapshots captures my attention. It shows my nephew Adel laughing, hands on his hips, in front of a mosque in Nazareth. I go back to the photo of Sihem posing before her childhood mosque. I know it's a recent photograph, less than a year old, because Sihem's got the purse I bought for her birthday last January. On the right, you can see the hood of a red car and a kid bending down to a dog. I go back to the photo of Adel. The red car's in this one, too, and so are the kid and the dog. So these two pictures were taken at the same time; the two subjects probably took turns with the camera. It takes me a little time to admit it. Sihem used to go to Nazareth regularly to spend time with her grandmother. She loved her native town. But Adel? I don't remember ever having seen him up there. That wasn't his environment. He often came to see us in Tel Aviv when his business affairs took him away from Bethlehem, but Nazareth? Did he range that far? I feel a constriction around my heart. A vague unease comes over me. I'm frightened by these two photographs. I try to imagine an excuse for them, a reason, a hypothesis—in vain. My wife never went out with a relative of ours without my knowing about it. She always told me where she'd been, whom she'd met, who had called her on the telephone. It's true that she appreciated Adel's humor and spontaneity, but the idea that she would meet him somewhere other than the house, somewhere other than Tel Aviv, without mentioning it to me—she just wasn't like that.

This coincidence exercises me. It overtakes me in the restaurant and spoils my dinner. It intercepts me when I'm back home. It keeps me awake, in spite of two sleeping pills. . . . Adel, Sihem . . . Sihem, Adel . . . the Tel Aviv–Nazareth bus. . . . She claimed it was an emergency and got off the bus and then climbed into a car that had been following the bus . . . an old cream-colored Mercedes. Just

like the one I caught a glimpse of in the abandoned warehouse in Bethlehem. "That belongs to Adel," Yasser told
me proudly. . . . Sihem was in Bethlehem, her last stop before the attack. . . . Too many coincidences.

I push off the covers. The alarm clock tells me it's five
o'clock in the morning. I get dressed, jump into my car, and
head for Kafr Kanna.

There's no one at the farm. A neighbor tells me that Sihem's grandmother was taken to the hospital in Nazareth
and that her nephew Abbas was with her. At the hospital,
I'm not allowed to see the patient, who's undergoing an
emergency operation. Cerebral hemorrhage, a nurse tells
me. Abbas is half-asleep on a bench in the waiting room.
When he sees me, he doesn't even get up. That's his character; he's as stiff as the trigger on an old carbine. A fifty-five-
year-old bachelor who's never left the farm, he's wary of
women and city dwellers, whom he avoids like the plague.
He'd rather work himself to death day after day than be under the obligation to sit down for a meal with someone who
doesn't smell of plowed furrows and sweat. He's a peasant
with a body carved out of oak, thin, sharp lips, and a ce-
ment head. He's wearing his mud-stained boots, his shirt
with the sweat stains around the armpits, and a pair of
rough, horrible pants that look as though they've been cut
from a tarpaulin. He gives me a succinct account: He found
Grandmother lying on the floor with her mouth open, he's
been at the hospital for hours, and he neglected to untie the
dogs. Grandmother's condition is more of a bother to him
than a cause for sadness.

We wait in the room until a doctor comes and tells us the operation is over. Grandmother's condition is stable, but her chances of pulling through are minimal. Abbas asks to be allowed to return to the farm. "I've got to feed the chickens," he grumbles, not really interested in the doctor's report.

He jumps into his rusty pickup truck and dashes off in the direction of Kafr Kanna. I follow him in my car. Only when he's finished with his various farm chores—that is, at the end of the day—does he notice that I'm still here.

He admits that he often saw Sihem in the company of the boy in the photograph. The first time was when he, Abbas, went back to the hairdresser's to give Sihem her purse, which she'd left on the seat of his truck. When he got there, he found Sihem and the boy in conversation. In the beginning, Abbas didn't think anything about it. But later, after he'd come across them together in several different places, he began to suspect something unseemly. But it was only when the boy in the photo dared to show up at the farm that Abbas threatened to split his skull with a pickax. This incident had very much offended Sihem. Afterward, Abbas says, she never set foot in Kafr Kanna again.

"That can't be true," I tell him. "Sihem spent the last two Eids with her grandmother."

"I'm telling you, she never came back after I told off that punk she was with."

Then, gathering my courage, I ask him what the nature of the relationship between my wife and the boy in the photograph was. At first, he's astonished by the naïveté of my question; he looks me up and down with a frozen grin of disappointment and irritation. "Do I have to draw you a picture, or what?"

"Do you have any sort of proof?"

"Some signs are unmistakable. I didn't need to catch them in each other's arms. The way they crept along the walls was enough for me."

"Why didn't you say anything to me?"

"Because you didn't ask me anything. And besides, I mind my own business, that's what I do."

At that precise moment, I loathe him as I've never loathed anyone in my life.

I get back in my car and roar off without a glance at the rearview mirror. I've got the accelerator pedal on the floor, and I don't even see where I'm going. The danger that I may miss a curve or plow into someone's trailer doesn't slow me down. In fact, I believe that's exactly what I want, but the road is cruelly deserted. My mother used to say to my father, "He who dreams too much forgets to live." My father paid her no heed. He never detected her disappointment in love or noticed her companionless solitude. There was something like an invisible membrane between those two, as thin as a lens, but it kept them at opposite ends from each other. My father had eyes only for his canvas, the same one that he painted summer and winter, repainting and painting over until the picture disappeared under layers of retouching; then he'd reproduce it on another easel, always the same painting, right down to the tiniest detail. My father was sure his *Madonna in Handcuffs* would rank with the Mona Lisa, and he believed it was going to open up his horizons and crown with laurels the prestigious rooms where he intended to exhibit it. It was because his vision was filled with this impossible dedication that he never noticed anything around him, neither the frustrations of a neglected wife nor the anger of a fallen patriarch. . . . Maybe that's what happened to me with Sihem. She was my canvas, my chief dedication. I saw only the joy she gave me and never suspected any of her sorrows, any of her weaknesses. . . . I didn't really *live* her. No, I didn't. If I had, I would have idealized her less and isolated her less. Now that I think about it, how could I have lived her when I never stopped *dreaming* her?

13.

————————

Mr. Jaafari. Someone's talking through an interminable series of subterranean galleries. . . . *Mr. Jaafari.* . . . The cavernous voice fades away under my babbling and then begins coming and going like an elusive leitmotiv, sometimes insistent, sometimes frightened. A chasm sucks me in and broods over me as I twirl slowly in the darkness. Then the voice catches me again and tries to haul me to the surface. . . . *Mr. Jaafari.* . . . A streak of light slashes through the dark, burning my eyes like a white-hot rapier.

"Mr. Jaafari."

I come to my senses, with my head in a vise.

A man is leaning over me, one hand behind his back, the other suspended a few centimeters from my forehead. His emaciated face, prolonged by a funnel-shaped chin, is completely unfamiliar to me. I try to reach some conclusions about my location. I'm lying on a bed. My throat is dry, and my body is a wreck. The ceiling over my head threatens to bury me. I close my eyes to contain the vertigo racking me, spinning me faster and faster. I force myself to regain my senses and get my bearings. Gradually, I recognize the picture on the opposite wall—a cheap reproduction of Van Gogh's *Sunflowers*—and take in the faded wallpaper and the dismal window, which looks out over the roofs of what seems to be a factory.

"What's going on?" I ask, propping myself up on one elbow.

"I believe you're unwell, Mr. Jaafari."

My elbow gives way and I fall back onto the pillow.

"You've been in this room for two days. You haven't left it since you got here."

"Who are you?"

"The hotel manager, sir. The chambermaid—"

"What do you want?"

"I want to be sure you're all right."

"Why?"

"You came to us two days ago. You took this room and locked yourself in. Now, some of our guests may do that from time to time, but . . ."

"I'm fine."

The manager straightens up and becomes obsequious. He doesn't know how to take my response. He walks around the bed and goes to open the window. A flood of cool air pours into the room, stinging me. I breathe deeply until my blood pounds in my temples.

With a mechanical gesture, the manager smooths the covers at my feet. He looks at me attentively, coughs into his fist, and says, "We have a good doctor, Mr. Jaafari. If you wish, we can call him."

"I'm a doctor," I say stupidly, extracting myself from the bed.

My knees knock together; I can't stand on my feet, and I drop onto the edge of the bed with my cheeks in my hands. Except for some rather ineffective briefs, I'm naked, and the manager is embarrassed. He murmurs something I don't catch and backs out of the room.

My ideas return to their places, one after another; my memory comes back to me whole. I remember leaving Kafr Kanna like a rocket, picking up a speeding ticket on the outskirts of Afula, and continuing on to Tel Aviv in a kind of trance. Night overtook me just as I was crossing the city limits. I stopped at the first hotel I came to. I didn't even consider going to my house, where I'd be back among all the lies of a lifetime. I spent the whole road trip cursing the world and myself; I kept the accelerator pedal pressed to the floor, and occasionally the ferocious screeching of the tires vibrated inside me like some apocalyptic scream. It was as if I was striving to break the sound barrier, to burst through the point of no return, to disintegrate along with my crumbled self-esteem. Nothing seemed capable of holding me anywhere anymore or reconciling me with tomorrow and tomorrow. And what tomorrows? Is there a life after perjury, a resurrection after the final insult? I felt so paltry, so ridiculous, that the thought of lamenting my fate would have finished me on the spot. When Abbas's voice came back to me, I made the engine howl until it nearly

came apart. I didn't want to hear anything but the squealing of the wheels in my barely controlled skids and the hissing of the bile eating away at my insides like an acid bath. I
had no excuse for myself, wasn't looking for one, didn't deserve any. I gave myself over entirely to my chagrin, which
desired me for itself alone and wanted me to embody it
from the roots of my hair to the tips of my toenails.

This is a shabby hotel. Its neon sign struggles to stay
lighted. I took a room the way you resign yourself to your
fate. After a scalding shower, I went to a bistro for dinner
and then got completely drunk in some squalid bar. It took
me hours to find my way back. As soon as I was in my room
again, without any warning, I sank into the abyss.

I have to use the wall for support on my way to the bathroom. My limbs are only halfway responsive. I feel nau-
seous, my vision is blurred, and I'm hungry; I have the
impression of moving inside a cloud. Two days asleep in
this foul-smelling room, without dreams and without memory; two nights spent wrapped up in these bedcovers as
though in a shroud. My God! What am I becoming?

The mirror shows me a tormented face blemished further by a growth of beard. Sallow circles bring out the
whites of my eyes and make my cheeks even hollower. I
look like a madman who's just come out of a fit.

I drink from the faucet at length, slip into the shower,
and stand motionless under the torrent of water until I recover some semblance of equilibrium.

The hotel manager comes and scratches on my door to
make sure I haven't fallen back into an alcoholic coma. He's

relieved when I growl at him and moves away soundlessly. Still woozy, I dress, leave the hotel, and find a place to eat.

Afterward, I go into a sunny little park. Amid the soothing rustling of the foliage, I fall asleep on a bench.

When I wake up, night has fallen. I don't know where to go or what to do with my solitude. I've forgotten my mobile phone at home, along with my watch. Suddenly, I'm afraid of being alone with myself. I no longer trust the man who didn't see his misfortune coming. At the same time, I don't feel ready to bear the scrutiny of other people. I tell myself it's a good thing I forgot my cell phone. I can't imagine talking to anyone in the state I'm in. Kim would aggravate my wounds; Navid might offer me the excuse I shouldn't use. On the other hand, the silence is killing me. In this deserted park, I feel alone in the world, like a shipwrecked person washed up on a fatal shore.

I go back to the hotel and realize I've forgotten my toilet kit and my pills. The telephone on the night table mocks me. But whom can I call? And what time is it? My panting breath fills the room. I'm not well; I feel myself slipping away somewhere, inexorably. . . .

And here I am, back in the street, all at once. I don't remember leaving the hotel, and I don't know how long I've been roaming around this neighborhood. No light in any window. The only sound is the drone of a distant engine, and then the night reclaims its rights over the sleeping city. . . . I see a telephone booth some distance away, next to the newsstand. My feet march me down there forcefully; my hand picks up the receiver; my fingers dial the number.

Who is it I'm calling? And what am I going to say to him? The telephone on the other end of the line rings five, six, seven times. Then there's a click, and a sleepy grumble in my ear: "Hello? Who is it? Do you have any idea what time it is? Me, I've got to work tomorrow." I recognize Yasser's voice, but I'm surprised he's answered the phone. Why him?

"It's Amin."

There's a silence, and then Yasser speaks again, still spluttering, but more calmly. "Amin? Is anything wrong?"

"Where's Adel?" I hear myself ask him.

"Do you know it's three o'clock in the morning?"

"Where's Adel?"

"How should I know? He's wherever his business has taken him. I haven't seen him for weeks."

"Are you going to tell me where he is, or do I have to come to your house and wait for him?"

"No!" he cries out. "Don't even think about coming to Bethlehem. The guys from the other day are looking for you. They say you tricked them. They say you're working for the Shin Bet."

"Where's Adel, Yasser?"

Another silence, longer than the preceding one. Then Yasser gives up and blurts it out: "Jenin. Adel's in Jenin."

"That's not the best place for business investments, Yasser. The town is under siege."

"Listen, I'm telling you the truth. The last I heard, he was in Jenin. I don't have any reason to lie to you. I'll let you know as soon as he returns, if you want. Do you mind telling me what this is all about? What is it about my son that makes you call me up at this hour?"

I hang up.

I don't know why, but I feel a little better.

———

The night clerk isn't best pleased at being dragged out of bed at three o'clock in the morning. The hotel closes at midnight, and I've forgotten the entry code. The clerk's a scrawny young man, probably a university student who spends his nights watching over other people's sleep to finance his education. He opens the door for me without enthusiasm and looks for my key, but he can't find it anywhere.

"Are you sure you dropped it off before you left?"

"Why would I burden myself with a room key?"

He plunges back behind the reception counter, rummages among the papers and magazines by the fax machine and the copier, and straightens up, empty-handed. "That's strange," he says.

Not fully awake, he has to think about where the duplicate keys might be. He says, "Are you sure you don't have the key on you, sir?"

"I'm telling you I don't have it," I say, slapping my pockets.

My arm stiffens: the key's in my pocket. I pull it out in confusion. The night clerk, visibly exasperated, suppresses a sigh, but he gets ahold of himself and wishes me a good night.

Since the elevator's out of order, I climb the stairs to the fifth floor before it occurs to me that my room's on the third, and I retrace my steps.

I don't turn on the lights in my room.

I undress, stretch out on the bed, and stare at the ceiling, which draws me in, little by little, like a black hole.

———

From the fifth day on, it becomes apparent that my wits are leaving me, one after another. My reflexes outstrip my intentions, and my clumsiness makes everything worse. By day, I remain closed up in my room, slumped in the chair or stretched out on the bed with my eyes rolled back, as if I were trying to sneak up on my hidden motives—because some strange ideas have been pestering me without letup: I think about engaging a real estate agency to sell my house, turning my back on the past, and exiling myself to Europe or even America. At night, I slip out like a predator and make the rounds of the seediest dives, certain that I won't run into any acquaintances or former colleagues in such places, where I myself have never been before now. The darkness of these polluted, smoky, rancid-smelling bars inspires in me a strange feeling that I'm invisible. Despite the lack of privacy—the drunks holding forth, the women looking enchanted—no one pays any attention to me. I take a table in a secluded corner where tipsy girls hardly ever venture and knock back glass after glass, steadily but calmly, until someone comes and tells me it's closing time.

Then I go to the same park, take the same bench, and sleep off the wine I've drunk, never getting back to the hotel before the first light of dawn.

Then, some time later, in a small restaurant, everything gets out of hand. The anger I've been brooding over for days finally bursts inside me. I've been expecting this. I've been too touchy, too wired; I knew I was going to short-circuit sooner or later. My words are intentionally brutal, my replies insultingly curt. I'm surly and impatient, and I react very badly when anyone looks at me too long. No doubt about it, I'm becoming someone else, someone unpredictable and fascinating at the same time. But this evening, in the little restaurant, I outdo myself. First of all, I don't appreciate the table they've given me. I want a discreetly placed table, but there's none available. I balk and then yield. Next, the waitress informs me there's no more grilled liver. She seems sincere, but I don't like her smile.

"I want grilled liver," I say obstinately.

"I'm very sorry, we've run out of grilled liver."

"That's not my problem. The menu outside says you've got grilled liver. That's what I came in for, and nothing else."

The sound of my raised voice interrupts the clicking of the forks. The other customers turn toward me.

I scream at them: "Why are you looking at me like that?"

The manager appears at once. He deploys all his professional charm to calm me down, but his superficial courtesy awakens my demons. I demand to be served some grilled liver at once. A wave of indignation runs through the room. Someone suggests, without mincing words, that the staff throw me out. The speaker is a gentleman of a certain age; he looks like a cop, or maybe a soldier in civilian clothes. I invite him to get fucked or throw me out himself. He accepts the invitation willingly and grabs me by the throat. The waitress and the manager try to stop the brute. A chair is knocked over in the uproar, which features cracking furniture and shouted abuse. The police arrive. Their commanding officer is a blond woman with an immense chest, a grotesque nose, and burning eyes. The brute explains to her how the situation degenerated. His assertions are borne out by the waitress and a high proportion of the customers. The officer requests that I step outside, where she asks to see my papers. I refuse to show them to her.

"He's completely drunk," one of her subordinates says.

"Put him in the car," the officer orders.

They hustle me into an automobile, take me to the nearest police station, and oblige me to present my papers and empty my pockets. They lock me in a cell where two drunks are sound asleep and snoring.

An hour later, a policeman comes to get me. He leads me to a window, where I'm handed back my personal effects, and then he accompanies me to the reception area. Navid Ronnen is there, leaning on a counter and looking glum.

"Well, look who it is, my guardian angel," I cry out disagreeably.

Navid dismisses the policeman with a movement of his head.

"How did you know I was in the tank?" I ask. "You've got your guys tailing me, or what?"

"Nothing of the sort, Amin," he says in a weary voice. "I'm relieved to see you standing upright. I was expecting the worst."

"Like what, for example?"

"A kidnapping, or even a suicide. I've been looking for you for days. And nights. As soon as Kim told me you'd disappeared, I sent out your name and description to all the hospitals and police stations. Where the hell have you been?"

"It doesn't matter." I turn to the policeman behind the counter. "May I go?"

"You're a free man, Mr. Jaafari."

"Thank you."

A hot wind is sweeping the street. Two cops are smoking and conversing, one of them propped against the wall of the station, the other sitting on the step of a police van.

Navid's car is pulled up against the curb across the street with its parking lights on. "What are you going to do now?" he asks me.

"Stretch my legs."

"It's getting late. Don't you want me to drop you off?"

"My hotel isn't far away."

"What do you mean, your hotel? You can't find your way home?"

"I'm quite comfortable at the hotel."

Looking stunned, Navid rubs his cheeks. "So where is this hotel of yours?"

"I'll take a taxi."

"You don't want me to give you a ride?"

"It's too much trouble. Besides, I need to be alone."

"Am I supposed to understand that—"

"There's nothing to understand," I say, cutting him off. "I need to be alone, period. That's all. That's clear, isn't it?"

Navid catches up with me at the corner. He has to pass me in order to put himself in my way. He says, "It's no good, what you're doing, Amin. I assure you, it's not. If you could see the state you've got yourself in."

"Am I doing anything wrong? Am I? Tell me how I'm doing wrong. Your colleagues were revolting, by the way. They're racists. The other guy started the fight, but I've got the appropriate face. That's why I'm guilty, not because I've been in a jail. I've seen enough for this evening. I just want to go back to my hotel now. I'm not asking for the moon, damn it! What's wrong with wanting to be alone?"

"Nothing," Navid says, putting a hand on my chest to stop me from moving forward. "Except that isolating yourself is a mistake. It can do you harm. Come on, Amin. You've got to pull yourself together. You're on the verge of flipping out. And you're wrong to believe you're alone. You still have friends you can count on."

"Can I count on you?"

My question surprises him. He spreads out his arms and says, "Of course."

I gaze at him. He doesn't turn his eyes away, but a fiber at the tip of his cheekbone twitches.

"I want to pass through the mirror," I mutter. "I want to go to the other side of the Wall."

He frowns and leans forward to look at me more closely. "Into Palestine?"

"Yes."

He pouts a little, turning toward the two cops who are observing us on the sly. He says, "I thought you took care of that problem."

"So did I."

"And what is it that's got you worked up again?"

"Let's say it's a question of honor."

"Your honor's intact, Amin. We're not guilty of the wrongs other people do to us, just the wrongs that we do."

"It's a hard pill to swallow."

"You don't have to."

"That's where you're wrong."

Navid takes his chin between his thumb and index finger and frowns mightily. He has a hard time picturing me in Palestine in my present depressed state and looks for a more subtle way of changing my mind. But he's run out of arguments, so he says, "It just isn't a good idea."

"I don't have any others."

"Where do you want to go, exactly?"

"Jenin."

"The town's under siege," he warns me.

"So am I. You haven't answered my question. Can I count on you?"

"I don't suppose there's any way of making you listen to reason."

"Reason? What might that be? I'm asking you whether I can count on you or not. Yes or no?"

He's embarrassed and saddened at the same time.

I dig in my pockets, find a crumpled package of cigarettes, pull one out, and put it in my mouth. Then I realize I don't have my lighter anymore.

"I don't have a light," Navid says apologetically. "Besides, you ought to stop smoking."

"Can I count on you?"

"I don't see how. You're going into dangerous territory, where I don't have any power and my good luck's not worth anything. I don't know what you're trying to prove. There's nothing for you up there. They're all blasting away at one another all the time, and stray bullets are causing more damage than pitched battles. I'm warning you: Bethlehem is a beach resort compared to Jenin."

He realizes his blunder and tries to recover—too late. His last sentence explodes in my head like a bomb. My words shake in my throat as I pounce on him: "Kim promised me not to say anything, and she always keeps her word. So if she didn't tell you, how do you know I went to Bethlehem?"

Navid's somewhat mortified, but nothing more. His face doesn't reflect any weakening of his will. "What would you have done in my place?" he asks in exasperation. "My wife's best friend turns out to be a suicide bomber. She caught us all off guard—her husband, her neighbors, the people closest to her. You want to know how and why? That's your right. But it's also my duty."

I can't get over it.

I'm paralyzed.

"Good grief!" I say.

Navid tries to come close to me. I raise my two hands, imploring him to stay where he is, and then I take the first side street and plunge into the night.

14.

———————

In Jenin, Reason has a mouth full of broken teeth, and it rejects any prosthesis capable of giving it back its smile. Besides, nobody smiles here. When shrouds and battle flags become the order of the day, the good humor of the past goes by the boards.

"And you haven't seen anything yet," Jamil says, as if reading my thoughts. "Hell's a rest home compared to what goes on here."

Nevertheless, I have seen many things since I passed to the other side of the Wall: small villages in a state of siege; checkpoints on every access road; larger roads littered with charred vehicles blasted by drones; cohorts of the damned, lined up and waiting their turn to be checked, pushed about, and often turned back; young soldiers, mostly beardless boys, losing patience and lashing out indiscriminately; protesting women, with nothing to ward off the blows of the rifle butts but their bruised hands; a few Jeeps

speeding across the plains while others escort Jewish set-
tlers, who go to their work as though passing through a
minefield.

"A week ago, it seemed like the end of the world," Jamil
adds. "Have you ever seen armor replying to slingshot fire,
Amin? Well, in Jenin, the tanks opened fire on the kids who
were throwing stones at them. Goliath stomping David,
everywhere you looked."

I'd had no idea that the state of decay was so advanced
here, and all hope so effectively dashed. Of course, I'm
aware of the animosities destroying brain cells on both
sides, and I know all about the obstinacy of the warring
parties, their refusal to reach an agreement, their devotion
to their own murderous hatred; but seeing the unbearable
with my own eyes traumatizes me. When I was in Tel Aviv,
I was on another planet. My blinders shielded me from taking in much of the tragedy devastating my country; the
honors I received hid the real level of the horrors that were
all around me, turning the Holy Land into a shambles. The
fundamental values of humanity are lying here, eviscerated;
the incense stinks of broken promises; prayers are lost amid
the sounds of weapons being cocked and sentinels' chal-
lenges.

"We can't go any farther," Jamil informs me. "We're
practically on the demarcation line. Just past the wrecked
patio on the left and you're on the firing range."

He shows me a heap of blackened stones. "Islamic Jihad
executed two traitors last Friday. Their bodies were exposed
over there. They swelled up like balloons."

I gaze around me. The neighborhood looks evacuated. The only people I see are a foreign television team and the armed guides who stand around them as they film the rubble. A 4×4 bristling with Kalashnikovs arrives out of nowhere, roars past us, and disappears around a turn, its tires screeching horribly; the cloud of dust it leaves behind takes a long time to disperse.

Some gunshots ring out, not far away, followed by a dead, unnerving calm.

Jamil backs to a traffic circle. He stops the car, stares down a silent street, weighs the pros and cons, and decides not to run unnecessary risks. "It's not a good sign," he says. "Not a good sign at all. I don't see any fighters from the al-Aqsa Martyrs' Brigades. Usually, there are two or three of them posted here to direct us. If they're all gone, it means they're setting up an ambush in this part of town."

"Where does your brother live?"

"A few hundred yards from that mosque. You see the damaged roofs on the right? He lives just on the other side. But to get there, you have to drive through the neighborhood, and it's infested with snipers. The worst is over, but fighting still flares up. Sharon's soldiers have occupied a good part of the town and closed off the main roads. They wouldn't even let us get close to them because the car might be booby-trapped. As for our fighters, they're extremely nervous, and they shoot before they ask for your papers. We picked a bad day to visit Khalil."

"What do you suggest?"

Jamil passes his tongue over his bluish lips. "I don't know. I wasn't expecting this."

Two Red Cross vehicles go past us, and we follow them at a distance. A shell explodes far away, then another one. Two helicopters are roaring around in the dusty sky with rockets armed and ready. We stay behind the two ambulances, proceeding very cautiously. Whole blocks of houses have been knocked down by tanks and bulldozers, others destroyed by dynamite. The land where they stood is littered with mounds of earth and scrap iron, where colonies of rats have encamped, waiting to consolidate their empire. Rows of ruins line former streets; the crippled facades stand silent, covered with cracks and graffiti. And everything— the piles of rubbish, the carcasses of vehicles crushed by tanks, the bullet-riddled fences, the suspense-filled squares— everything evokes horrors I thought had been abolished, and I feel a growing certainty: The old demons have made themselves so desirable that none of the possessed wants to be free of them.

The two ambulances turn into a field full of dazed ghosts. "The survivors," Jamil explains. "The houses that were knocked down were theirs. Now they're gathering here."

I don't say anything; I'm frightened. My hand trembles as I take out my pack of cigarettes. Jamil says, "Will you give me one?"

The ambulances stop in front of a building where some mothers are waiting impatiently with their children clinging to their skirts. The drivers jump out, open the back doors of their vehicles, and start handing out food on all sides, creating the beginnings of a crush.

Jamil manages to get through a series of shortcuts, back-

ing up every time a gunshot or a suspicious silhouette
freezes our blood.

At last, we reach some parts of town that have been rel-
atively spared by the fighting. Militants—some in camouflage, some wearing hoods—bustle about frantically. Jamil
explains that he's got to leave his car in a garage; from now
on, we're going to have to trust to our legs.

We walk up innumerable little streets teeming with angry
people before we get a glimpse of Khalil's hovel. Jamil
knocks on the door several times; no response.

A neighbor tells us that Khalil and his family left a few
hours ago for Nablus.

"What a drag!" Jamil cries. "Did he say exactly where in
Nablus?"

"He didn't leave an address. Did he know you were coming?"

"I couldn't reach him!" Jamil says, furious at having
come all this way for nothing. "Jenin's cut off from the
world. Can you tell me why he left for Nablus?"

"He just left, that's all. Why should he stay here? We've
got no running water and nothing to eat, and no one can
sleep, day or night. If I had some relative or friend willing
to take me in somewhere else, I'd do the same thing."

Jamil asks me for another cigarette.

"What a drag!" he says again. "I don't know anybody in
Nablus."

The neighbor invites us to go to his house and rest for a
while. "No, thanks," I say. "We're in a hurry."

Jamil tries to figure out our next move, but his disappointment distorts his thoughts. He squats down in front of his brother's door and puffs nervously on his cigarette, his jaws clenched.

All of a sudden, he leaps to his feet. "What are we going to do?" he says. "I'm not interested in hanging around these parts. I've got to get back to Ramallah and return the car to its owner."

I'm annoyed, too. Khalil was my only lead. When last heard from, Adel was staying at Khalil's place. I was hoping that Khalil would lead me to him.

We're cousins, Khalil, Jamil, and I. I don't know Khalil very well—he's ten years older than I am—but Jamil and I were quite close when we were teenagers. We haven't seen much of each other in recent years, mostly because our professions are incompatible—I'm a surgeon in Tel Aviv; he's a security guard in Ramallah—but whenever he happens to be passing through town, Jamil makes a stop at my house. He's a good man, an affectionate, selfless family man. He's fond of me, and he remembers our shared childhood with unfailing tenderness. When I told him I was planning to visit him, he immediately asked his boss for a few days off so he could attend to me. He knows about Sihem; furthermore, Yasser has told him about my exciting adventures in Bethlehem and mentioned that people suspect me of working for the Israeli intelligence services. Jamil didn't want to hear anything about that. He threatened never to speak to me again if I stayed in Ramallah with anyone else but him.

I spent two nights there, waiting for a mechanic to fix my car. Jamil had to ask another cousin to loan us his vehicle and promise to return it by evening. He was planning to drop me off at his brother Khalil's house and head back to Ramallah at once.

"Is there a hotel?" I ask the neighbor.

"Of course. More than one. But with all these journalists, they're full. If you want to wait for Khalil at my place, you won't disturb me. There's always an available bed in a true believer's house."

"Thanks," I say. "We'll manage."

———

We find a room in a sort of inn not far from Khalil's house. After asking for payment in advance, the clerk accompanies me to the second floor; Jamil stays downstairs. The clerk shows me a room the size of a storage closet, furnished with a moribund bed, a rudimentary night table, and a metal chair. He points out the toilets at the end of the hall and an all-purpose emergency exit and leaves me to my fate. I put my bag on the chair and open the window, which looks out over the center of town. Off in the distance, a group of boys are stoning the Israeli tanks and then scattering when the soldiers open fire; the whitish smoke of tear gas bombs spreads through narrow streets filled with dust; a crowd gathers around the body of someone who has just been shot down. I close the window and rejoin Jamil downstairs. Two disheveled journalists are sleeping on a sofa, their equipment unpacked and spread out around them. The clerk informs us that there's a little bar at the end of the street on the right if we want a drink or a snack. Jamil asks me to let him go back to Ramallah. "I'll pass by Khalil's place before I leave," he says. "I'll give the neighbor the address of your hotel so he can contact you as soon as Khalil returns."

"That's fine. I won't leave the hotel. For one thing, I don't believe there are any good tourist walks around here."

"You're right. Stay quietly in your room until someone comes to fetch you. Khalil will surely come back today, or tomorrow at the latest. He never leaves his house unoccupied like this."

He gives me a hug. "Don't do anything foolish, Amin."

————

After Jamil leaves, I go to the bar and smoke a few cigarettes while having a cup of coffee. Some armed teenagers wearing green scarves wrapped around their heads and bulletproof vests covering their chests enter the bar. They place themselves in a corner, where they're soon joined by a French television team. The youngest fighter comes over and explains that they're about to conduct an interview and politely invites me to clear off.

I go back to the hotel and watch pitched battles from the window in my room. My heart sinks at the spectacle before my eyes. Jenin. It was the big city of my childhood. Since the tribal lands were just about twenty miles from town, I often accompanied my father when he went to Jenin to offer his canvases to various sleazy art merchants. At the

time, Jenin seemed as mysterious to me as Babylon, and I
loved to pretend that the mats I saw there were flying car-
pets. Then, when puberty made me more attentive to the
swaying hips of the women as they strolled along, I learned
to go to Jenin alone, like a grown-up. Jenin: with its telltale
airs of the big provincial town aping the great cities, its re-
lentless crowds, which made it always resemble a souk during Ramadan, its shops like Ali Baba's cave, where trinkets
did their best to dissemble shortages, and its narrow, fra-
grant alleyways, populated by street kids who seemed like
barefoot princes. But there was also Jenin's picturesque
side, which fascinated pilgrims in a former life, the aroma
of its bread, which I've never come across anywhere else,
and its good nature, always vivacious despite so many misfortunes. What's happened to the little touches that were its
charm and its signature, that made its girls' modesty as
fatal as their cheekiness and its old men venerable despite their impossible temperaments? The reign of the absurd has ravaged everything, even the children's faces;
everything is sunk in an unhealthy grayness. You'd think
you were in some forgotten reach of limbo, haunted by
amorphous souls, by broken creatures, half ghosts, half
damned, trapped in events like flies in paint, their faces distraught, their eyes rolled back, turned toward the night, so
miserable that not even the great sun of As-Samirah can
light them.

Now Jenin's nothing but a disaster area, a giant mess. It
has nothing worth saying and seems as unfathomable as the
smiles of its martyrs, whose portraits are posted on every

street corner. Mutilated by the multiple incursions of the Israeli army, punished and revived by turns to make the pleasure last longer, the town lies sprawling amid its curses, out of breath and short on incantations. . . .

Someone knocks on the door.

I awaken from my reverie. The room is plunged in darkness. My watch says it's six o'clock in the evening.

The person at the door announces, "Mr. Jaafari, you've got a visitor."

A boy is waiting for me at the desk. He's too large for his multicolored clothing. He's got to be on the young side of eighteen, but he's trying to look older. His fine-featured face is edged with stray hairs, which he's passing off as a beard.

"My name is Abu Damar," he says formally, introducing himself. "That's my nom de guerre. I'm someone you can trust. Khalil sent me to fetch you."

He embraces me, mujahideen-style.

I follow him through a neighborhood in turmoil, where the sidewalks have vanished under layers of rubble. This area must have been evacuated by the Israeli troops only a short time ago, because the streets still show the marks of the tanks' caterpillar tracks, as a torture victim bears the fresh traces of his ordeal. Kids in a pack, sounding like a stampede, rush past us and disappear, yelling, into an alleyway.

My guide walks too fast for me; from time to time, he's obliged to stop and wait.

"This doesn't look like the way," I point out.

"It's going to be night soon," he explains. "Certain sectors are off-limits at night. To avoid mistakes. We're very disciplined in Jenin. Instructions are followed to the letter. Otherwise, we wouldn't be able to hold out."

He turns to me and adds, "As long as you're with me, you're not running any risk. This is my sector. In a year or two, I'll be in command here."

We come to an unlit cul-de-sac. An armed silhouette is standing guard in front of a gate. The boy pushes me toward it.

"Here's our doctor," he says, proud of having accomplished his mission.

"Very good, kid," the sentinel says. "Now go back home and forget about us."

The boy's a little mortified by the guard's peremptory tone. He takes his leave and hastens to disappear into the darkness.

The guard invites me to follow him into a patio, where two paramilitaries are cleaning their rifles by the light of a flashlight. A tall man in a parachutist's jacket too small for him stands at the entrance to a large room full of camp beds and sleeping bags. He runs this outfit. He's got a spotted face and white-hot eyes, and he's not overjoyed to see me.

"You're out for a little revenge, Doctor?" he asks me point-blank, so abruptly that it takes me a minute to recover my wits.

I say, "What?"

"You heard me," he replies, leading me into a concealed

room. "The Shin Bet has sent you to stir us up so we'll come out of our holes and give their drones target practice."

"That's a lie."

"Shut up," he says menacingly, slamming me into a wall. "We've had our eye on you for a good long time. Your holiday in Bethlehem caused quite a sensation. What exactly is it that you want? Your throat slit in a gutter? A public hanging in the square?"

All at once, this man inspires a feeling of stark terror in me.

He sticks the barrel of his pistol in my side and forces me to kneel down. One of his fighters, whom I didn't see when I came in, pulls my hands behind my back and handcuffs me without any brutality at all, as though he were performing an exercise. I'm so surprised by the turn that events have taken and the confident ease with which I stepped into the trap that I can hardly believe what's happening.

The man squats down to look at me closely. "End of the line, Doctor. Everybody gets off. You shouldn't have pushed things this far. We have no patience with assholes here, and we don't let them ruin our lives."

"I've come to see Khalil. He's my cousin."

"Khalil got the hell out as soon as he got wind of your visit. He's not stupid. Do you have any idea of how much you fucked up in Bethlehem? Because of you, the imam of the Grand Mosque had to move out of it. Now we must suspend all operations there while we try to see if our networks have been uncovered. I don't know why Abu Mukaum agreed to meet you, but it was a very bad initia-

tive on his part. He, too, has had to move. And now you're
in Jenin for more of the same?"

"I'm not working for anybody. No one's manipulating
me."

"Is that right? They arrest you after your wife's attack;
then, three days later, they turn you loose, just like that, no
charges, no indictment. They did everything but apologize
for the inconveniences they caused you. Why? Because of
your pretty eyes? I admit, we'd be almost tempted to believe
that, except no one's ever seen such a thing before. No pris-
oner of the Shin Bet has ever been set free without having
first sold his soul to the devil."

"You're wrong."

He grabs me by the jaws and presses my face to keep my
mouth open. "The good doctor has a grudge against us.
His wife died *because of us*. But she was so happy in her
gilded cage, wasn't she? She ate well, slept well, enjoyed
herself. She lacked nothing. And then, look, a bunch of
mental cases turn her away from her happiness and send
her to—how did you put it?—to 'blow herself away.' The
good doctor lives next door to a war, but he doesn't want to
hear a word about it. And he thinks that his wife shouldn't
worry about it, either. Ah well, the good doctor is wrong."

"They released me because I had nothing to do with the
attack. No one recruited me. I simply want to know what
happened. That's why I'm looking for Adel."

"But what happened is clear. We're at war. Some people
take up arms; others twiddle their thumbs. And still others
make a killing in the name of the Cause. That's life. But as

long as everyone stays in his proper place, there's no problem. Difficulties begin when those who are living the good life come and lecture those who are up to their necks in shit. Your wife chose her side. The happiness you offered her smelled of decay. It repulsed her, you get it? She didn't want your happiness. She couldn't work on her suntan while her people were bent under the Zionist yoke. Do I have to draw you a picture to make you *understand*, or do you refuse to look reality in the face?"

He stands up, shaking with rage, pushes me against the wall with his knee, and leaves the room, locking the door behind him.

A few hours later, still handcuffed, I'm gagged and blindfolded and thrown into the trunk of a car. I believe this is the end. They're going to take me out to some field and execute me. But what really disturbs me is my docility, the way I submitted to them. A lamb would have defended himself better. When the trunk lid slammed down, it took away the last shreds of my self-esteem at the same time that it cut me off from the rest of the world. To have come all this way, to have made this arduous journey, just to wind up in the trunk of a car, like a common bundle! How could I fall so low? How could I tolerate being treated like this without lifting so much as a finger? A feeling of impotent rage sends me far back into the past. I remember a morning when Grandfather was driving me to see a quack dentist in his old jalopy, and he skidded on a rut and knocked over a mule cart. The fallen driver rose to his feet and began calling Grandfather every name he could think of. I was waiting for the patriarch to fly into an epic rage in his turn, the sort of rage he used when he wanted to reduce recalcitrant members of the tribe to trembling, and how disappointed I was to see my own personal centaur, the person I revered so much that I confounded him with a divinity, apologizing *effusively* and picking up his kaffiyeh after the muleteer snatched it out of his hands and threw it on the ground. I was so sad that my cavity stopped hurting. I was seven or eight. I didn't want to believe that Grandfather would let anyone humiliate him like that. I was outraged and impotent, and every cry of the muleteer lowered me down another notch. All I could do was to look at my idol collapsing before my eyes, like a sea captain watching his ship slip beneath the waves. And the sadness that takes hold of me when the lid of the trunk comes down is exactly the same. I'm ashamed for submitting to so many insults so passively—so ashamed that I don't care what fate awaits me. I'm not anything anymore.

15.

They shut me up in a blind cave, with no window and no light.

"Not exactly luxury accommodations," says the man in the parachute jacket, "but the service is top-notch. You have no chance of escaping from here, so don't try anything clever. If it was up to me, you'd already be starting to stink. Unfortunately, I'm part of a hierarchy, and it doesn't always share my qualms."

My heart almost stops beating when he slams the door behind him.

I embrace my knees and remain still.

The next day, they come to get me, and here I am in the trunk of a car again, handcuffed, my head in a sack and a gag in my mouth. After a long, bumpy ride, they take me out and throw me on the ground. Then they pull me to my knees and remove the sack. The first thing my eyes focus on is a large stone, stained with clotted blood and riddled with the traces of bullets. Death has a strong stench in this place. A lot of people must have been executed here. Someone puts the barrel of a rifle against my temple. "I know you have no idea where the Kaaba is, but it's always a good idea to say a prayer." The metallic bite devours me from head to feet. I'm not afraid, but I'm trembling so much, my teeth are chattering violently. I close my eyes, gather up whatever dignity I have remaining, and wait for them to get it over with. The spit and crackle of a walkie-talkie saves me at the last moment; my executioners are ordered to postpone their dirty job and return me to the place where they're holding me.

Once again, the darkness, except this time I'm alone in the world, without any shadow watching over me and without any memories, except for this sickening fear in my guts and the trace of the rifle barrel on my temple.

The following day, they come and get me again. At the end of our walk, there's the same big soiled rock, the same stage business, the same spitting walkie-talkie. I realize that what's going on is a crudely faked execution; they're trying to make me crack.

After this, no one comes to disturb me anymore.

I spend six days and six nights in this pestilential rat hole, fair game to fleas and cockroaches, living on cold soup and grinding my vertebrae against a pallet hard as a gravestone.

I was expecting muscular interrogations, torture sessions, or things of that nature; instead, nothing. Some galvanized teenagers, brandishing their submachine guns like trophies, have been charged with guarding me. If by chance they bring me something to eat, they don't speak a word, ignoring me haughtily.

On the seventh day, a commander under heavy escort pays me a visit in my cave. He's a young man in his thirties, somewhat frail-looking, with a face like a knife blade scorched on one side and two yellowish eyes. He's wearing faded combat fatigues and carrying a Kalashnikov assault rifle slung across his back.

He waits for me to get to my feet, hands me a pistol, and steps back a couple of paces. "It's loaded, Doctor," he says. "Shoot me."

I lay the gun on the floor.

"Shoot me. It's your right. Afterward, you can go back home and start your life over again. No one here will touch a hair of your head."

He comes closer and tries to put the pistol back in my hand.

I refuse to take it.

"Conscientious objector?" he asks.

"Surgeon," I say.

He shrugs, stuffs his pistol into his belt, and speaks to me confidentially: "I don't know whether I've succeeded, Doctor, but I wanted you to experience, physically and mentally, the kind of hatred that's eating away at us. I have requested and obtained a detailed report on you. I'm told that you're a decent man and an eminent humanist, and that you've got no reason to wish people ill. So it was difficult for me to make you understand my point of view without stripping you of your social rank and dragging you through the mud. Now that you've touched, if only with your fingertips, the dirty realities your professional success has spared you, I have a chance of making myself understood. Existence has taught me that a man can live on love and fresh water, on crumbs and promises, but he can never survive insults. And insults are all I've known since I came into the world. Every morning. Every evening. That's all I've seen for my whole life."

He makes a small hand gesture. One of his men throws a sack at my feet.

"I've brought you some new clothes. Paid for out of my own pocket."

I'm having trouble following him.

"You're free to go, Doctor. You requested a meeting with Adel. He's waiting for you in a car outside. And your great-uncle would like to receive you in the patriarch's house. If you don't want to see him, that's not a problem. We'll tell him you were prevented by unforeseen circumstances. We've prepared a bath for you, and a better meal than what you've been getting. If that's all right with you."

I remain on my guard, unmoving.

The commander squats down, opens the sack, and shows me some clothes and a pair of shoes to prove his good faith.

"So how have you spent the last six days in this stinking cellar?" he asks, straightening up with his hands on his hips. "I daresay you've learned how to hate. If not, this experiment has been useless. I shut you up in here so you

could develop a taste for hatred and a desire to act on it. I
haven't humiliated you as a matter of form. I don't like hu-
miliating people. I've felt humiliation, and I know what it
is. When a person has been scorned, when his self-esteem
has been wounded, all tragedies become possible. Especially if he recognizes that he's impotent, with no means of
restoring his dignity. I believe that the best school for hatred
is located in this very place. The instant when you really
learn to hate is the one in which you become aware of your
impotence. It's a tragic moment—the most appalling, the
most abominable of all."

He grabs me forcefully by the shoulders.

"I wanted you to understand why we've taken up arms,
Dr. Jaafari, why our teenagers throw themselves on tanks
as though they were candy boxes, why our cemeteries are
filled to overflowing, why I want to die with my weapons in
my hand, and why your wife went and blew herself up in a
restaurant. There's no worse cataclysm than humiliation.
It's an evil beyond measure, Doctor. It takes away your taste
for life. And until you die, you have only one idea in your
head: How can I come to a worthy end after having lived
miserable, and blind, and naked?"

He notices that his fingers are hurting me and removes
his hands.

"No one joins our ranks for the pleasure of it, Doctor.
All the young men you've seen, the ones with slingshots as
well as the ones with rocket launchers, loathe war unspeak-
ably. Because every day, enemy fire carries off one of them.
They'd like to be respectable, too; they'd like to be surgeons

or pop singers or film actors, ride around in fine cars and live their dreams every day. The problem, Doctor, is that other people deny them those dreams. Other people are trying to confine them to ghettos until they're trapped in them for good. And that's the reason why they prefer to die. When dreams are turned away, death becomes the ultimate salvation. Sihem understood this, Doctor. You must respect her choice and let her rest in peace."

He starts to withdraw, then stops and speaks again. "There are only two extreme moments in human madness: the instant when you become aware of your own impotence and the instant when you become aware of the vulnerability of others. It's a question of accepting one's madness, Doctor, or suffering it."

Whereupon he pivots on his heels and departs. His lieutenants fall in behind him.

I remain as though planted in the middle of my cell, facing the wide-open door, through which I see a patio white with sunlight. The rays ricochet into my brain. I hear several vehicles start up and drive off, and then silence. I think I'm dreaming, but I don't dare pinch myself. Is this another trick?

A silhouette appears in the doorway. I recognize who it is right away—the squat, thick body, the sloping shoulders, the short, slightly bowed legs: It's Adel. I don't know why, but when I see him coming to me in my dark hole, a sob shakes me from my head to my feet.

"Ammu?" he says in a ravaged voice.

He comes toward me, taking little steps, as though he were venturing into a bear's den.

"Uncle? It's me, Adel. I was told you were looking for me. Well, here I am."

"You took your time."

"I wasn't in Jenin—it was only yesterday evening that Zakaria ordered me to return here. I arrived less than an hour ago. And I didn't know I was coming back for you. What's going on, Ammu?"

"Don't call me uncle. Times have changed since I welcomed you in my home and treated you like a son."

"I see," he says, lowering his head.

"How can you see anything, when you're not even twenty-five? Look at the state you've reduced me to."

"It's not my fault. It's not anybody's fault. I didn't want her to blow herself up, but she was determined. Even Imam Marwan was unable to dissuade her. She said she was a full-blooded Palestinian, and she didn't see why she should let others do what she ought to do herself. I swear to you, she wouldn't listen to anybody. We told her she was much more useful to us alive than dead. She'd given us a lot of help in Tel Aviv. We held all our most important meetings at your house. We disguised ourselves as plumbers or electricians and went there with our equipment. We drove service vans so as not to arouse suspicion. Sihem put her bank account at our disposal—we would deposit money into it for the Cause. She was the keystone of our Tel Aviv section."

"And Nazareth?"

"Yes, Nazareth, too," he says without any embarrassment at all.

"And where did you hold your meetings in Nazareth?"

"No meetings in Nazareth. We did fund-raising there.

After we made the rounds of our benefactors, Sihem assumed the responsibility of transporting the money to Tel Aviv."

"And that's all?"

"That's all."

"Really?"

"What do you mean?"

"What kind of relationship did you have with her?"

"We were comrades in arms."

"Just comrades? Well, a Cause is certainly a convenient thing to have."

Adel scratches the crown of his head. It's impossible to tell whether he's perplexed or desperate. The light's coming from behind him, and I can't see the expression on his face.

I say, "Abbas has a different take on the matter."

"Who's he?"

"Sihem's uncle. The one who wanted to smash your skull with a pickax at Kafr Kanna."

"Ah! The nutcase."

"He's perfectly sane. He knows exactly what he's doing, and what he's saying. He saw you two hanging out together in Nazareth."

"So what?"

"He suggests that some signs are unmistakable."

At this particular moment, I don't give a damn about the war, good causes, heaven and earth, or martyrs and their monuments. It's a miracle that I'm still standing. My heart's beating like mad in my chest; my guts are awash in the corrosive juice of their own decay. My words outstrip my anxieties, flashing out from the core of my being like incendiary sparks. I'm afraid of every word that goes out of my mouth, afraid it'll come back on me like a boomerang, loaded with something that will annihilate me on the spot. But my need for clarity, my need to clear my mind, is stronger than anything else. It's as though I were playing Russian roulette: my fate isn't important, since the moment of truth is going to decide between us once and for all. I don't care about finding out exactly when Sihem sank into suicidal militancy or knowing whether I wronged her somehow, whether I contributed in one way or another to her ruin. All that has been pushed into the background. What I want to know first and foremost, what has supreme importance in my eyes, is whether or not Sihem was cheating on me.

Adel sees, at last, what I'm getting at. He's outraged.

"What do you mean by that?" he says in a strangled voice. "No, it's not possible. What are you trying to say? Are you insinuating that . . . that . . . No! You can't be! How dare you?"

"She certainly kept her political activity a secret from me."

"That's not the same thing."

"It is the same thing. When you lie, you're cheating."

"She didn't lie to you. I forbid you—"

"You? You've got the nerve to forbid me—"

"Yes, I forbid you!" he shouts, decompressing like a spring. "I will not permit you to soil her memory. Sihem was a pious woman. And you can't cheat on your husband without offending the Lord. It would make no sense. Once you've chosen to give your life to God, that means you've *re-nounced* the things of this life, all earthly things, without exception. Sihem was a saint. An angel. I would have been damned just for looking at her too long."

And I believe him, my God! I believe him. His words save me from my doubt, from my misery, from myself. I drink them in to the dregs; I fill myself with them. The black clouds above my head go whirling away dizzily, leaving a clear sky. A gust of air blows through me, chasing away the fumes that were poisoning me inside and brightening my blood. My God! I'm *saved*! And now that I've brought the salvation of humanity down to my own infinitesimal person, now that my honor has been spared, I lose sight of my anger and my rage and I'm almost tempted to forgive everything. My eyes fill with tears, but I don't allow them to spoil this hypothetical reconciliation with myself, these intimate reconnections that I celebrate alone somewhere in my flesh and my spirit. However, it's all too much for a man as reduced as I am; my knees buckle, and I collapse onto the pallet with my head in my hands.

I'm not ready to go out onto the patio. It's too soon for me. I prefer to stay in my cell a little while longer, long enough to pull myself together and find my place in this sequence of revelations, which seem to branch off in every direction. Adel sits down beside me. His arm hesitates for a long time before wrapping itself around my neck—a gesture that repulses me and overwhelms me, but which I don't reject. He starts to cry—remorse or sympathy? In either case, it's not what I was expecting. Do I really expect any-

thing at all from a man like Adel? It seems highly unlikely.
We have radically different ideas about what people should
expect from one another. For him, Paradise is at the end of
a man's life; for me, it's at the tips of your fingers. For him,
Sihem was an angel; for me, she was *my* wife. For him, angels are eternal; for me, they're dying of our wounds. No,
he and I have hardly anything to say to each other. It's a
lucky break that he's even noticed I'm in pain. His sobs
shake me harder and harder, down to the deepest part of
my being. Without my realizing it, and without my being
able to justify it, my hand gets away from me and grasps his
in consolation. . . . And then we talk and talk and talk, as
if we're striving for total exorcism. When Adel went to Tel
Aviv, it wasn't for his business; he was there to supply the
local cell of the Intifada with funds. He took advantage of
my reputation and my hospitality to place himself above
suspicion. One day, by accident, Sihem found a briefcase
hidden under the bed he was using. When she took hold of
it, some documents and a handgun fell out. Upon his return, Adel realized right away that his hiding place had
been discovered. He thought about raising the alarm and
vanishing. He even thought about killing her so nothing
would be left to chance. In fact, he was planning Sihem's
"accidental death" when she came into his room with a
wad of shekels. "That's for the Cause," she said. Adel says
it was months before he started to trust her. Sihem wanted
to join him in the resistance. The cell put her to the test,
and she convinced them. Why didn't she tell me anything?

When I ask him this, he says, "Tell you what? She

couldn't tell you anything; she didn't have the right. And furthermore, she had no intention of letting anyone get in her way. A commitment like this, you keep quiet about it. If you've taken oaths that are to be observed in absolute secrecy, then you don't cry them from the rooftops. My mother and father think I'm in business. The two of them are waiting for me to make my fortune so I can raise them up out of their misery. They don't know I'm a militant; they don't know a thing about my activities in the Intifada. They're militants, too, in their way. They wouldn't hesitate to give their lives for Palestine—but they wouldn't give their child. That's not normal. Children are their parents' survival, their little piece of eternity. When they hear the news of my death, they'll be inconsolable. I've taken full measure of the grief I'm going to cause them, but that will be just one more sorrow to add to a long list. In time, their mourning will be over, and they'll wind up forgiving me. Sacrifice isn't a duty just for other people. If we accept that other people's children die for ours, we must accept that our children die for other people's; otherwise, it wouldn't be fair. And that's where you can't follow, Ammu. Sihem was a woman, not just your woman. She died for others."

"Why her?"

"Why not her? Why should Sihem remain outside the history of her people? What did she have more or less than the women who sacrificed themselves before her? It's the price of freedom."

"She *was* free. Sihem was free. She had everything she wanted. I deprived her of nothing."

"Freedom isn't a passport issued by the authorities, Ammu. Going where you want to go isn't freedom. Having enough to eat isn't success. Freedom's a deep conviction, the mother of all certitudes. Now, Sihem wasn't so sure she deserved her good fortune. You lived under the same roof and enjoyed the same privileges, but you weren't looking in the same direction. Sihem felt closer to her people than she did in your image of her. Maybe she was happy, but not happy enough to be like you. She didn't hold a grudge against you for prizing so highly the honors you were showered with, but that wasn't the happiness she wanted to see in you; she found it a little indecent, a bit incongruous. It was as if you were firing up a barbecue in a burned-out yard. You saw only the barbecue; she saw the rest, the desolation all around, spoiling all delight. It wasn't your fault; all the same, she couldn't bear sharing your blindness anymore."

"I just didn't see it coming, Adel. She seemed so happy."

"It was you. You wanted so much to make her happy that you refused to think about what might throw a shadow on her happiness. Sihem didn't want your kind of happiness. She came to see it as morally questionable, and the only way for her to atone was to join the ranks of the Cause. It's a natural progression when you're the child of a suffering people. There's no happiness without dignity, and no dream is possible without freedom. The fact of being a woman doesn't disqualify or exempt a resistance fighter. Men invented war; women invented resistance. Sihem was the daughter of a people noted for resistance. She was in a very good position to know exactly what she was doing, Ammu. She wanted to *deserve* to live, *deserve* her reflection in the mirror, *deserve* to laugh out loud, not just to enjoy her good fortune. Same goes for me. I could go into business and get rich quicker than Onassis. But how can I accept blindness in order to be happy? How can a man turn his back on himself without coming face-to-face with his own negation? You can't water a flower with one hand and pluck it with the other. When you put a rose in a vase, you don't restore its charm; you denature it. You think you're beautifying your room, but, in fact, all you're doing is disfiguring your garden."

I come up against the clarity of his logic like a fly striking a windowpane; I see his message plainly, but I can't possibly absorb it. When I ponder what Sihem did, I find it unconscionable and inexcusable. The more I think about it, the less I accept it. How could she have reached the point where she would do such a thing? "And it can happen to anybody." Navid told me. "Either it falls on your head like a roof tile or it attaches itself to your insides like a tapeworm. Afterward, you no longer see the world in the same way." Sihem must have been carrying that hatred inside her forever, long before she met me. She grew up among the oppressed, as an orphan and an Arab in a world that pardons neither. She must necessarily have had to bow very low, like me, except that she could never straighten up. The memory of certain compromises imposes a heavier burden than the weight of the passing years. To go so far as to pack herself with explosives and walk out to her death with such determination, she must have been carrying around a wound so awful, so hideous, that she was too ashamed to show it to me; the only way for her to be rid of it was to destroy it and herself together, like a possessed man who jumps off a cliff in order to triumph over his demons and his weakness at once. It's true that she hid her scars admirably well. Maybe she tried to disguise them, without success, and all it took was a simple little click to awaken the beast that was sleeping inside her. When did that happen, that click? Adel didn't ask her, and probably even Sihem herself didn't know when it was. One more atrocity on the TV news, some mistreatment on the street, a random insult: When you've got hate inside of you, it doesn't take much to push you past the point of no return. . . . Adel's talking, talking and smoking like a fiend. . . . I realize I'm not listening to him anymore. I don't want to hear anything else. I don't fit in the world he's describing. There, death is an end in itself. For a physician, that's too much to swallow. I've brought so many patients back from the next world that I started taking myself for a god. And when I lost a patient, when one of them slipped away from me on the operating table, I became the vulnerable, sad mortal I've always refused to be. I don't recognize myself in what kills; my vocation is to be on the side of what saves. I'm a surgeon. And Adel's asking me to come to terms with death as an ambition, a dearest wish, a legitimacy; he's asking me to accept what my wife did— that is, to accept exactly what my physician's calling forbids me even in the most desperate cases, even if it's euthanasia. That's not what I'm looking for. I don't want to be proud of being a widower, I resent having to give up the happiness that made me a husband and a lover, a master and a slave, and I don't want to bury the dream that made life worth living as it will never be for me again.

I push away the sack at my feet and stand up. "Let's go, Adel."

He's a bit miffed at being cut off so abruptly, but he gets up in his turn.

"You're right, Ammu. This isn't the best place to talk about such things."

"I don't want to talk about them at all. Not here and not anywhere else."

He acquiesces. "Your great-uncle Omr knows you're in Jenin. He's asking to see you. If you don't have enough time, that's no problem. I'll explain it to him."

"There's nothing to explain, Adel. I've never renounced my family."

"That's not what I meant."

"You were just thinking out loud."

He avoids my eyes.

"You don't want to have a bite to eat first? Or take a bath?"

"No. I don't want anything from your friends. I don't appreciate their cuisine or their hygiene. I don't want their clothes, either," I add, kicking the sack out of my way. "I've got to go back to my hotel and pick up my things, assuming they haven't been distributed to the needy."

The sunlight on the patio assaults my eyes, but the sun does me good. The fighters have left. The only person I see is a smiling young man standing beside a dusty automobile.

"This is Wissam," Adel says. "Omr's grandson."

The young man throws his arms around my neck and hugs me tightly. When I step back to have a look at him, he hides behind his smile, embarrassed by the tears filling his eyes. Wissam! I knew him when he was a squalling baby in diapers, hardly bigger than my fist, and look at him now, a head taller than me, with a mustache like an inscription and one foot already in the grave. It's always touching to see a person his age adrift, except when he drifts in the direction Wissam's chosen. The pistol peeking out from under his belt breaks my heart.

"Take him to his hotel first," Adel orders him. "He's got some stuff to collect there. If the clerk's forgotten where he put them, you refresh his memory for him."

"You're not coming with us?" Wissam says, surprised.

"No."

"You were up for it a little while ago."

"I changed my mind."

"Fine with me. Whatever you say. See you tomorrow, maybe."

"Who knows?"

I expect Adel to come and embrace me, but he stays where he is, head bent down, hands on his hips, worrying a pebble with the tip of his shoe.

"Okay, see you soon," Wissam says.

Adel looks at me with eyes full of darkness.

That look!

The same look Sihem gave me that morning when I dropped her off at the bus terminal.

"I'm really very sorry, Ammu."

"So am I."

He doesn't dare approach me. For my part, I don't give him any help, much less make the first move myself. I don't want him imagining things; I want him to know that my wound is incurable. Wissam opens the door for me, waits for me to settle in my seat, and then runs around the car and gets in on the driver's side. The car makes a circle in the little parking area, nearly grazes Adel—who stands there as though paralyzed, sunk in his thoughts—and turns into the street. I'd like to see that look again, to examine it; I don't turn around. As we drive downhill, the street branches off into a multitude of narrow side streets. The noises of the town reach me; the movement of the crowds exhilarates me; I lay my head on the back of the seat and try to think about nothing.

At the hotel, they give me back my things and allow me to take a bath. I shave and change my clothes, and then I ask Wissam to drive me out to see the lands where my ancestors came from. We leave Jenin without a hitch. For some time now, the fighting has stopped, and a good part of the Israeli forces have withdrawn from the town. Several teams of TV reporters and cameramen are scouring the rubble, looking for some horror they might profitably record. Our car crosses an interminable series of fields before we reach the shabby road that leads to the orchards of the patriarch. I let my gaze run over the plains like a child running after his imaginings. But I can't stop thinking about the way Adel looked at me, and about the darkness enveloping him. He made a strange impression on me, a feeling like a flag at half-mast. I can still see him standing there on that white-hot patio. He's not the funny, generous Adel I used to know; he's someone else, someone tragic, driven like a wolf whose ambition doesn't ever project past the next meal, the next prey, the next mass killing. He smokes his cigarette as if he'll never smoke another, he talks about himself as though he no longer exists, and the shadows of funeral parlors darken his eyes. It's obvious: Adel doesn't belong to the living anymore. He has irreversibly turned his back on the future, into which he refuses to survive, as if he's afraid it may disappoint him. He has chosen the status that, according to him, best suits his character: the status of martyr. That's the way he wants to wind up: at one with the Cause he defends. Stone slabs already bear his name; his family's memory bristles with his feats of arms. If he has nothing on his conscience, if he doesn't reproach himself in any way for having set Sihem on the road to the supreme sacrifice, if war has become his only chance of gaining self-esteem, that's all because he's dead himself and he's just waiting to be laid in the earth so he can rest in peace.

I believe I've arrived at my destination. The route I took has been terrible, and I don't have the impression that I've reached anything or learned anything redemptive. At the same time, I feel liberated; I tell myself that my suffering is over, and from now on nothing can catch me off my guard. This painful search for the truth has been my personal voyage of initiation, my very own. Am I going to reconsider the order of things now? Am I going to call it into question, reposition myself in relation to it? Of course, but I won't feel as though I'm contributing to anything major. For me, the only truth that counts is the one that will help me one day to pull myself together and go back to my patients. Because the only battle I believe in, the only one that really deserves *bleeding* for, is the battle the surgeon fights, which consists in re-creating life in the place where death has chosen to conduct its maneuvers.

16.

————————

Omr, the chief elder of the tribe, the last survivor of an era whose sagas were the bedtime stories of our childhood; Omr, my great-uncle, the man who passed through the last century like a shooting star, so bright and swift that his prayers were never able to catch up with him; there he is, in the patriarch's courtyard, smiling at me. He's happy to see me again. His deeply creased faced quivers with a joy so poignant, you would think him a child reunited with his father after a long separation. A hajji many times over, he has known glory and honors, traveled to many countries, and ridden through exalted lands on the backs of celebrated purebreds. He fought in the troops led by Lawrence of Arabia—"that pallid jinni come from the foggy north to stir up the Bedouins against the Ottomans and sow discord among Muslims"—and served in King Ibn Saud's royal bodyguard before falling in love with an odalisque and fleeing the Arabian Peninsula with her.

Then restless wandering, followed by a period of decline, put an end to their union. Abandoned by his muse, he dragged his kit from principality to sultanate in search of exploitable opportunities, committed the odd act of brigandage here and there, and then became, in succession, an arms trafficker in San'a and a rug merchant in Alexandria before being gravely wounded in the defense of Al-Qods in 1947. In my first memories of him, he's limping around because of the bullet in his knee; later, I remember him bent over a cane after the heart attack he suffered the day he watched Israeli bulldozers laying waste to the patriarch's orchards in order to make way for a Jewish colony. Today, I find him terribly diminished, with a cadaverous face and bleary eyes, little more than a bundle of bones huddled in a wheelchair.

I kiss his hand and kneel at his feet. His tapered fingers rummage in my hair while he tries to gather enough breath to tell me how much my return to the family home fills him with happiness. I lay my head on his chest, just as I did as a spoiled child when I came to him weeping for favors others had refused me.

"My doctor," he says in his shaky voice. "My doctor."

Faten, his thirty-five-year-old granddaughter, is at his side. I wouldn't have recognized her in the street. It's been such a long time. When last I saw her, she was a skittish kid, always picking fights with her cousins and then running off as though she had the devil on her heels. The family news I used to get sporadically in Tel Aviv pictured her as chronically unlucky. People with wicked tongues call her "the Virgin Widow." It's certainly true that Faten has had more than her share of misfortune. Her first husband died in their wedding procession, which came to a sudden end when the automobile they were riding in suffered a freakish blowout, followed by a collision; her second fiancé was killed in a clash with an Israeli patrol two days before the wedding night. Immediately, gossiping shrews inferred that she was accursed, and no suitor has ever knocked at her door again. She's a sturdy, uncouth young woman, formed by a lifetime of demanding household tasks and the austere existence of the enclaved villages. Her greeting is robust and her kisses noisy.

When the eldest of the tribe consents to let go of my hand, Wissam, who has already picked up my bag, shows me to my room. I'm asleep before my head touches the pillow. Toward evening, Wissam comes to wake me up. He and Faten have installed the table under the arbor. They've spared no expense for this meal. Old Omr, sunk in his wheelchair, sits at the head of the table, not taking his eyes off me for a second. We have dinner outside, the four of us. Wissam tells amusing stories from the front until late in the night. Omr's chin has dropped onto his chest, but his eyes laugh, looking up from under their lids. Wissam is a piece of work; it's hard for me to believe that such a shy boy has developed such a hilarious sense of humor.

I go back to my room, intoxicated by his tales.

The next morning, I'm on my feet just as night begins to pull her black skirts away from the first touch of dawn. I've slept like a child. I may have had some fine dreams, but I don't recall any of them. I feel fresh, cleansed. Faten's already got Omr out on the patio; I see him through the window, hieratic on his throne, like a convalescent totem. He's waiting for the sun to rise. Faten's just finished preparing some flat cakes for later, and now she serves me breakfast in the living room: coffee and milk, olives, hard-boiled eggs, various fruits, and slices of buttered bread dipped in honey. I eat alone—Wissam's still in bed. From time to time, Faten comes in to see whether I need anything. After my meal, I join Omr on the patio. He squeezes my hand tightly when I lean down to kiss him on the top of his forehead. If he doesn't say very much, it's because he wants to savor entirely every instant I offer him. Faten goes to the henhouse to feed the chickens. Every time she passes in front of me, she gives me the same smile. Despite the harshness of farm life and the cruelties of fate, she's hanging on. Her eyes look deserted and her movements are graceless, but her smile has jealously kept a trace of self-conscious affection.

"I want to take a walk," I say to Omr. "Who knows, I may find the copper button I lost somewhere around here more than forty years ago."

Omr nods but forgets to release my hand. His old eyes, reddened by sandstorms and adversity, shine like dirty jewels.

I cut through the kitchen garden, plunge into part of what remains of the orchard—a cluster of skeletal trees— looking for the trails we blazed in my childhood. The paths of yesteryear have disappeared, but the goats, perhaps less inspired but no more carefree than we were, have made new ones. I spot the hill I used to charge down in one of my periodic assaults on the general tranquillity. The cabin my father turned into his studio has fallen in; one wall has refused to abandon its post, but the rest is a mere ruin, completely rotted by the rains. I come upon the little wall behind which a band of cousins and I would plot ambushes against invisible armies. Part of the wall is cracked, its exposed insides filled with weeds. It was in this exact spot that my mother buried my stillborn puppy. My grief was so great that she wept along with me. My mother . . . a charitable soul who's disappearing off the coast of my memory; a soul lost forever in the murmur of the ages. I sit on a large stone and remember. I was no sultan's son, but what I see in my mind's eye is a prince, his arms spread like a bird's wings, flying over the misery of the world like a prayer over a battlefield, like a song that breaks the silence of those who can't take it anymore.

Now the sun breaks in on my thoughts. I rise to my feet and climb the hill, which is topped by a few shaggy trees. I scramble up the slope until I'm standing on the crest; in the time of the happy wars, this place was my watchtower. When I stood here in those days, I could see so far that with a little bit of concentration, I could glimpse the edge of the world. Today, there's a hideous great wall, built to further who knows what pernicious design, thrusting up incongruously into what was my sky when I was a child, a thing so obscene that the dogs prefer lifting their legs on brambles to pissing at its foot.

"Sharon's reading the Torah backward," a voice says, addressing my back.

An old man wrapped in faded but clean robes is standing behind me. He's got a hoary mane and a dour expression, and he leans on a cudgel as he eyes the great rampart blocking the horizon. I think of Moses staring at the Golden Calf.

"The Jew wanders because he can't stand walls," he says, without paying any attention to me. "It's not by chance that Jews have built a wall for the express purpose of moaning in front of it. Sharon's reading the Torah backward. He thinks he's protecting Israel from its enemies, but all he's really doing is enclosing it in another ghetto, less terrifying, of course, but equally unjust. . . ."

He turns to me at last. "Forgive me for disturbing you. I saw you coming up the path, and I took you for an old friend who's no longer with us, a man I miss. You have his silhouette, his way of walking, and—now that I see you close-up—some of his features. Would you perhaps be Amin, the son of Redwan the painter?"

"I would indeed."

"I was sure of it. It's amazing how much you resemble him. For a moment, I took you for his ghost."

He holds out a gnarled hand. "My name is Shlomi Hirsh, but the Arabs call me 'Zeev the Hermit.' There was some old-time ascetic by that name. I live in the hut up there, beyond the orange trees. Once upon a time, I worked as a

wholesaler for your patriarch. After he lost his lands, I re-
invented myself as a charlatan. Everyone knows I don't
have any more power than the chickens I sacrifice, but no
one seems to care. People still come to me and order up
miracles I have no hope of performing. I promise better days
for a few miserable shekels; since that's not exactly enough
to make my fortune, none of my clients holds it against me
if my prophecies miss their mark."

I shake his hand. He says, "Are you sure I'm not disturbing you?"

"Not anymore," I assure him.

"Very good. Not too many people come up this way,
not these days. Because of the Wall. It's really hideous,
the Wall, isn't it? How can people build such monstrosi-
ties?"

"Its hideousness isn't just a question of architecture."

"Of course not, but, frankly, they should have been
able to do better than this. A wall? What's it supposed to
mean? The Jew is born as free as the wind, as indomitable
as the Judean desert. Why did he mark the boundaries of
his homeland so carelessly that it was nearly taken from
him? Because for a long time he believed that the Promised Land is, first and foremost, the land where there's
no wall to keep him from seeing farther than his cries can
carry."

"And the cries of the others? What does he do about
those?"

The old man bows his head, picks up a bit of earth, and
crumbles it between his fingers. " 'What to me is the multi-

tude of your sacrifices?' says the Lord. 'I have had enough of burnt offerings . . .' "

"Isaiah 1:11," I say.

The old fellow gives me an admiring look. "Bravo," he says.

" 'How the faithful city has become a harlot, she that was full of justice!' " I recite. " 'Righteousness lodged in her, but now murderers.' "

" 'O my people, your leaders mislead you, and confuse the course of your paths.' "

" '. . . the land is burned, and the people are like fuel for the fire; no man spares his brother. They snatch on the right, but are still hungry, and they devour on the left, but are not satisfied; each devours his neighbor's flesh.' "

" 'When the Lord has finished all his work on Mount Zion and on Jerusalem he will punish the arrogant boasting of the king of Assyria and his haughty pride.' "

"So all Sharon has to do is behave himself, *amen*!"

We both burst out laughing.

"You astonish me," he declares. "Where did you learn all those verses from Isaiah?"

"Every Jew in Palestine is a bit of an Arab, and no Arab in Israel can deny that he's a little Jewish."

"I couldn't agree more. So why so much hate between relatives?"

"It's because we haven't learned much from the prophets and hardly anything about the elementary rules of life."

He nods his head sadly. "Then what's to be done?" he asks.

"First of all, give God back his freedom. He's been hostage to our bigotries too long."

A car is heading in our direction from the farm, trailing a long cloud of dust.

"That's surely for you," the old man announces. "People who come to pick me up ride only donkeys."

I offer him my hand, bid him farewell, and walk down the hillside to the trail to meet the car.

———

There's a crowd in the patriarch's house. Aunt Najet is there in person; she was at her daughter's in Tubas, but she came back at once as soon as she heard of my return to the family home. She's ninety now, but she hasn't slowed down a bit. She's always been solid on her feet, with flashing eyes and precise gestures. As the patriarch's youngest wife and only widow, she's the mother of all of us. When my real mother was about to scold me, all I had to do was cry out Aunt Najet's name and I'd be spared. Her tears run down onto my shirt. Cousins, uncles, nephews, nieces, and other relatives patiently wait their turn to embrace me. No one resents me for having gone far away and stayed there a long time. They're all happy to see me again, to have me to themselves, even if only long enough for a hug; they all forgive me for having ignored them for years and years, for having preferred gleaming buildings to dusty hills, broad avenues to goat paths, glitz and flash to the enduring, simple things of life. Surrounded by all these people who love me, and realizing that I have nothing but a smile to share with them, I measure how impoverished I've become. When I turned my back on these tormented, stifled lands, I thought I was breaking away for good. I didn't want to be like my family, to be subjected to the same misery and nourished by the same stoicism. I remember always trotting behind my father as he forged ahead, carrying his canvas like a shield and brandishing his paintbrush like a lance, determined to pursue his unicorn through a land where all the legends are depressing. Every time an art merchant shook his head, he erased the two of us. It was horrible. My father never gave up; he was convinced that, sooner or later, the wished-for miracle was going to occur. His failures infuriated me, and his perseverance gave me strength. And it was because I never wanted my fate to depend on a commonplace nod of the head that I renounced my grandfather's orchards, my childhood games, even my mother—that seemed the only way to make an epic destiny for myself. I was clearly unqualified for any other kind. . . .

Wissam has slaughtered three sheep to provide us with a *meshwi* worthy of the good old days. The reunions are all very touching; after awhile, I can hardly stand. Our whole family history comes back to me at a gallop, as magnificent as a troop of mounted warriors on parade. I'm introduced to frightened kids, new in-laws, future relatives. Some neighbors show up, as well as old acquaintances and a few friends of my father, including a couple of aging rascals. The feast is still going strong at the break of dawn.

On the fourth day, the patriarch's house returns to its habitual serenity. Faten sees to the chores. Aunt Najet and Uncle Omr pass their days on the patio, watching the mosquitoes dancing above the kitchen garden. A telephone call refocuses Wissam, who asks our permission to return to Jenin. He puts some things in a pack and then embraces the old folks and his sister Faten. Before leaving us, he tells me how lucky he feels to have met me "in time." I don't grasp what "in time" means, but I'm uneasy as I watch him depart. Nevertheless, I don't regret this sojourn among my family. Their warmth consoles me; their generosity re-assures me. I divide my days between the farm, where I keep the eldest of the tribe and Hajja Najet company, and the hill, where I meet old Zeev and listen to his hilarious stories about the credulity of the simple folk who are his clients.

Zeev's a fascinating character, a bit crazy, but wise, a kind of outcast saint who prefers to take things as they come, undifferentiated and at random, the way a person might take the next train, the idea being that every new discovery is enriching, even for one whose adventures tend to turn out badly. If it were up to him, he'd gladly trade his Mosaic rod for a witch's broom and amuse him-self with casting spells as therapeutic as the miracles he promises to the wretches who come to beg his mercy, mis-taking his destitution for abstinence and his marginaliza-tion for asceticism. I learn a lot about other people as well as myself in his company. His sense of humor makes trials and tribulations easier to bear; his sobriety keeps reality at a distance, for all its broken promises and dashed hopes. All I have to do is listen to him, and my worries fade away. When he launches into one of his torrential theories concerning the mad rage and the empty vanities of mankind, nothing can hold him back; he carries everything before him, starting with me. "A man's life is worth much more than any sacrifice, no matter how great," he declares, looking me in the eye. "For the greatest, the most just, the noblest cause on earth is the right to live. . . ." I find this man delightful. He's got the ability to resist being overwhelmed by events and the decency not to yield to the blows of misfortune. His empire is the hut he lives in, his feasts the meals he shares with people he likes, his glory a simple thought in the minds of those who will survive him.

We talk for hours on end, sitting on a big rock on the crest of the hill, our backs turned to the Wall and our eyes stubbornly fixed on the few orchards still standing on tribal land.

But one night, after I've taken my leave of him, trouble catches up with me.

The patio is filled with women dressed in black. Faten sits to one side, her head in her hands. Her sobs smother her moans, filling the farm with evil omens. A few men are chatting near the henhouse—relatives, neighbors.

I don't see the old man anywhere.

Has Uncle Omr died?

"He's in his room," a cousin informs me. "Hajja Najet is with him. He took the news very hard."

"What news?"

"Wissam. He died in action today. He filled his car with explosives and drove into an Israeli checkpoint."

The soldiers invade the orchard at daybreak. They arrive in machines covered with wire netting and surround the patriarch's house. Soon a tank transporter brings in a bulldozer. The commanding officer asks to see the eldest of the tribe. Since Omr's not well, I represent him. The officer informs me that as a consequence of the suicide operation carried out by Wissam Jaafari against an army checkpoint and in accordance with the instructions he's received from his superiors, we have half an hour to evacuate the dwelling so that he can proceed to destroy it.

"What do you mean?" I protest. "You're going to destroy the house?"

"Sir, you have twenty-nine minutes."

"It's out of the question. We're not going to let you destroy our house. What's the meaning of this? The people who live here, where do you expect them to go? There are two old people here, both of them well past ninety, trying to do the best they can in the few days remaining to them. You don't have the right. This is the patriarch's house, the most important center of the whole tribe. You have to leave here. At once."

"Twenty-eight minutes, sir."

"We're staying inside. We're not going to budge."

"That's not my problem," the officer says. "My bulldozer's blind. Once it starts, it keeps going to the end. You've been warned."

"Come on," Faten says, pulling my arm. "These people have no more heart than their machines do. Let's salvage what we can and get out."

"But they're going to destroy the house!" I shout.

"What's a house when you've lost a country?" she says with a sigh.

Some soldiers get the bulldozer off the tank carrier. Others keep at bay the neighbors who've started to arrive. Faten helps the old man drop into his wheelchair and pushes him to a sheltered spot in the courtyard. Najet doesn't want to take anything with her. "Those things belong with the house," she says. "In ancient times, the lords were buried with their earthly goods around them. This house deserves to keep its belongings. It'll be a fading memory, like a dream."

The soldiers oblige us to gather on a shabby mound some distance from their work site. Omr is sunk deep into his wheelchair—I don't think he realizes what's going on; he looks at the agitation around him without really seeming to see it. Hajja Najet stands behind him with as much dignity as she can muster; Faten's on his left and I'm on his right. The bulldozer bellows, spewing a thick cloud from its smokestack. As it pivots on itself, its steel tracks tear ferociously at the ground. The neighbors move past the security cordon set up by the police and join us in silence. The Israeli officer orders a group of his men to make sure there's no one remaining in the house. After he's certain that the house is empty, he gives a signal to the driver of the bulldozer. At the moment when the low wall surrounding the property collapses, a wave of rage washes over me, sending me running toward the machine. A soldier steps in my way; I shove him aside and keep charging toward the monster that's about to annihilate my family history. "Stop!" I shout. "Stop!" shouts the officer. Another soldier intercepts me. The butt of his rifle smashes into my jaw, and I drop down like an unhooked drapery.

————

I've stayed on the mound all day long, contemplating the debris of what was once, under a twinkling sky light-years ago, the castle where I was a barefoot little prince. My great-grandfather built it with his own hands, stone by stone; many generations flourished there, wider-eyed than the horizon; many hopes were nourished by those gardens. One bulldozer was enough to reduce all eternity to dust in a few minutes.

Toward evening, while the sun is barricading itself behind the Wall, a cousin comes looking for me. "It's no use staying here," he says. "What's done is done."

Hajja Najet has gone back to her daughter in Tubas.

The eldest of the tribe has found refuge in a great-grandson's house not far from the orchards.

Faten has immured herself in an impenetrable silence. She's chosen to stay with Uncle Omr in his great-grandson's hovel. She's always taken care of the old man, and she knows how demanding that task is. Without her, Omr wouldn't make it. In the beginning, other members of the

family agreed to take care of him, but he wound up neglected. That's why Faten decided to live in the patriarch's
house. Omr was her baby. But when the bulldozer went
away, it took Faten's soul with it. Now she sits lifelessly,
silently, with a dazed look on her face, like a shadow forgotten in a corner, waiting to melt into the night.

One evening, she goes back to the wasted orchard on
foot, her loosened hair hanging down her back—she who
has never been known to take off her head scarf—and
stands there the whole night, looking at the ruins under
which the essential part of her existence lies buried. When
I go out to get her, she refuses to come back with me.
Not one tear falls from her empty eyes, which are glazed in
that unmistakable way I've learned to fear. The next day,
she's disappeared without a trace. We move heaven and
earth to find her, but she's vanished. When the great-
grandson sees that I'm stirring up the neighboring villages,
he, fearing that things may get worse, takes me aside and
confesses: "I drove her to Jenin. She kept on insisting. In
any case, no one can do anything about it. It's always been
like this."

"What are you saying to me?"

"Nothing."

"Why did she go to Jenin? Who's she staying with?"

Omr's great-grandson shrugs his shoulders.

As he goes away, he says, "These are things people like
you don't understand."

When he says that, I understand.

I take a taxi back to Jenin and surprise Khalil at home.

He thinks I've come to have it out with him. I calm him down and explain that I just want to see Adel. Adel comes at once. I tell him that Faten has disappeared and let him know what I suspect she's up to.

"No woman has joined our ranks this week," he assures me.

"See what you can find out from Islamic Jihad or the other groups."

"That would be a waste of time. We're already having trouble agreeing on basics. Besides, no one has to account to anyone else. Everyone conducts his holy war the way he sees fit. If Faten's made up her mind, it's useless to try to bring her back. She's of age and perfectly free to do what she wants with her life. And with her death. There aren't two weights and two measures, *Doctor.* If you agree to take up arms, you have to agree that others may do the same. Each of us has a right to share in the glory of battle. You don't choose your destiny, but it's good to choose your end. It's a democratic way of giving fate the bird."

"I beg you, please find her."

Adel's upset. He shakes his head and says, "You still don't understand a thing, Ammu. But now I have to run. Sheikh Marwan's going to arrive any minute. He's giving a sermon in a little under an hour at the neighborhood mosque. You should come and listen to him."

That's it, I tell myself: Faten's probably in Jenin to receive the sheikh's blessing.

———

The mosque is full to bursting. Militiamen are lined up out-side, protecting the sanctuary. I take up a position on a nearby street corner and keep an eye on the part of the mosque reserved for women. The latecomers—some of them wrapped in black robes, others wearing brightly colored head scarves—are hurrying to reach the prayer hall through a concealed door in the rear of the mosque. No sign of Faten. I go around a block of buildings in order to approach the concealed door, where a fat lady is standing guard. She's scandalized to see me in the vicinity of that part of the sanctuary, where even the militiamen are too modest to show themselves.

"The men's entrance is on the other side," she informs me sternly.

"I know, sister, but I need to speak to my niece, Faten Jaafari. It's an emergency."

"The sheikh's already in the *minbar*."

"I'm very sorry, sister. I have to talk to my niece."

"And how am I supposed to find her?" she says, get-ting irritated. "There are hundreds of women inside, and the sheikh's about to begin his sermon. I can't very well snatch the mike away from him. Come back after the prayer."

"Do you know her, sister? Is she here?"

"What? You're not even sure she's here, and you come bothering us at a time like this? Go away or I'll call the guards."

I have no choice but to wait until the prayer's over.

I go back to my spot on the street corner, where I've got a good view of the mosque and the wing reserved for women. Imam Marwan's spellbinding voice, sovereign in the silence that has fallen on the neighborhood, booms from loudspeakers outside the building. It's practically the same speech I heard in the illegal cab I took that day in Bethlehem. From time to time, enthusiastic outcries salute the orator's lyrical flights.

A speeding vehicle screeches to a halt in front of the mosque; two militiamen get out, brandishing walkie-talkies. This looks serious. One of the men points an agitated finger toward the sky. Others leap out and consult for a while and then go off to find someone in charge. They return with the man in the parachutist's jacket, my former jailer. He puts a pair of binoculars to his eyes and scrutinizes the sky for several minutes. Movement begins on the perimeter of the sanctuary. Militiamen start running in every direction; three of them race toward me and pass me by, panting. One shouts authoritatively to the others, "If we don't see a helicopter, that means it's a drone." I watch them charging down the street as fast as they can. Another vehicle stops in front of the mosque. The occupants shout something to the man in the parachute vest, the vehicle backs up with an unnerving roar, and they speed away toward the square. The sermon is interrupted. Someone takes the microphone and asks the faithful to remain calm, because it could be a false alarm. Two 4×4s come hurtling up as some members of the congregation begin to evacuate the premises. They're blocking my view of the women's side of the mosque. I can't go around the block without the risk of missing Faten should she exit through the concealed door. I decide to pass in front of the main entrance, go through the crowd, and come out directly in front of the women's wing of the mosque. "Please move out of the way," one of the militia guards shouts. "Let the sheikh pass." The faithful elbow one another, hoping to get a better look at the sheikh or touch a part of his *kamis*. When the imam appears in the doorway of the mosque, a surge from behind me pushes me into the midst of the crowd. I'm being crushed by the enraptured throng and try in vain to break free. The sheikh plunges into his vehicle, waving with one hand from behind the bulletproof glass while his two bodyguards take their places on either side of him. And then . . . but there's nothing more. Something resembling a lightning bolt streaks across the sky and bursts like a giant flare in the middle of the roadway; the shock wave strikes me full force; the crowd whose frenzy held me captive disintegrates. In a fraction of a second, the sky collapses, and the street, fraught with the fervor of the multitude a moment ago, turns upside down. The body of a man, or perhaps a boy, hurtles across my vertiginous sight like a dark flash. What's going on? A surge of dust and fire envelops me, flinging me into the air with a thousand other projectiles. I have a vague sensation of being reduced to shreds, of dissolving in the blast's hot breath. . . . A few yards—or light-years—away, the sheikh's automobile is ablaze. Two blood-covered specters try to drag the imam out of the con-flagration. With their bare hands, they pull apart the flam-ing vehicle, break the windows, tear off the doors. . . . I can't get up. . . . An ambulance wails. . . . Someone bends over my body, gives me a summary examination with his stethoscope, and goes away without looking back. I see him stoop before a heap of charred flesh, take its pulse, and then make a sign to some stretcher-bearers. A man comes to me, picks up my wrist, and lets it fall again. "This one's a goner." In the ambulance that carries me off, my mother smiles at me. I try to reach out and touch her face, but no part of me obeys my wishes. I'm cold, I feel bad, I'm in pain. The ambulance pulls up howling at the entrance to the hospital. Stretcher-bearers open the doors. They lift me out and put me down in a corridor, right on the floor. Nurses step over me, running in every direction. Gurneys loaded with the wounded, with horror, pass back and forth in a dizzying ballet. I wait patiently for someone to come and take care of me. I don't understand why no one's spending any time at my bedside. They stop, they look at me, and they go away—that's not normal. Other bodies are lined up on both sides of mine. Some have small groups of relatives around them; the women scream and weep. Others are unrecognizable and can't be identified. The only person who kneels down beside me is an old man. He speaks the name of the Lord, puts his hand on my face, and closes my eyes. All at once, all the lights and all the sounds of the world fade away. Absolute terror seizes me. Why has he closed my eyes? When I can't reopen them, I understand: That's it, then; it's all over; *I am no more*. . . .

In a final effort, I try to regain control of myself; not a fiber in me stirs. There's nothing besides that cosmic sound humming around me, penetrating me bit by bit, already annihilating me. . . . Then, suddenly at the very bottom of the abyss, an infinitesimal glimmer of light. It quivers, approaches, slowly takes shape; it's a child, a running child; his fantastic strides drive back the impenetrable darkness around him. *Run*, cries his father's voice, *run*. . . . An aurora borealis rises over festive orchards; the branches of the trees immediately begin to bud, to blossom, to bend under the weight of their fruit. The child runs through the wild grass, heading for the Wall. It collapses like a big cardboard box, broadening the horizon and exorcising the fields, which extend over the plains as far as the eye can see. . . . *Run*. . . . And the child runs, laughing all the while, his arms spread out like a bird's wings. The patriarch's house rises from its ruins; its stones shed their dust and return to their places in a magic dance; its walls rise up; tiles cover its ceiling beams once more. Grandfather's house is standing upright again, more beautiful than ever. The child runs faster than pain, faster than fate, faster than time. . . . *And dream*, the artist calls to him. *Dream that you're beautiful, happy, and immortal*. . . . As though delivered from his torments, the child runs along the crest of the hills, flapping his arms like wings, his little face radiant, his eyes glittering with joy, and leaps for the sky, swept away by his father's voice: *They can take everything you own—your property, your best years, all your joys, all your good works, everything down to your last shirt—but you'll always have your dreams, so you can reinvent your stolen world.*